About the Author

Some people remember every detail of their lives, right back to the day they were born. Others can't recall what they were doing even last week. For the rest of us, the past is a rich mix of our own memories plus other people's. And if there are gaps, we invent something and believe it might have been true. That's what I did with this story about growing up fifty years ago and longing for love.

I had fun but there were some profoundly sad events too. However, learning to understand the sweetness of grief, even to welcome those memories of loss which ebb and flow, became part of who I am, and of who my siblings are. Whenever we are together, we still discuss our collective childhood as if it all happened yesterday.

Our chaotic family wasn't unique. Other children have suffered, and survived, as we did, supported by infuriating adults who proved their love by sticking around, even during the toughest times.

Rachel Anderson

Look out for other titles in the Moving Times trilogy

Grandmother's Footsteps
Stronger than Mountains

Also by Rachel Anderson

Blackthorn, Whitethorn
The Flight of the Emu
Pizza on Saturday
Red Moon

Other titles published by Hodder Children's Books

The Glittering Eye
Cherry Heaven
The Diary of Pelly D
L. J. Adlington

The Carbon Diaries 2015
Saci Lloyd

RACHEL ANDERSON

*Hodder
Children's
Books*

A division of Hachette Children's Books

Contents

ONE

Down the Garden Path

My eldest sister and I lay in the grass under the twisty old apple tree.

'I'm thinking about love,' she said.

'So am I.'

'He'll come this afternoon,' she said. 'In a white sports car.'

'White? You sure?' I'd had a daft idea that the sports car of our dreams would be black. I said, 'Hey, listen. There's this kit I've been reading about. The do-it-yourself car kit. So you can build your own Alfa Romeo Spyder. I'm sure it's black.'

The kit cost three thousand pounds. If I had the money to buy the kit, if I knew how to put it together (which would include some soldering skills and an understanding about the electrics), if I learned how to drive, and if I was at last old enough to have a licence, I could speed us both away to find life and love with big L's. I got sixpence a week pocket money. So did my sister. Our quaint, yet kindly mother considered this perfectly adequate.

'But listen girls, it's what *I* had from *my* mother! And you know that your granny has always been very fair.'

'But Mum, that was in the 1920s!'

These days, it was enough to buy six lemon sherbert dabs, or six liquorice bootstrings, or two Wagon Wheels, or three HB pencils, or two ruled exercise books with multiplication tables printed on the back cover, or one reel of Sylko sewing thread, 100 yards long, in any colour the village store had in stock.

My sister said, 'Definitely white. It's more bridal.'

People liked to say she was artistic but in my opinion she was often really quite prosaic.

'Well, the colour's not that important, is it?' I said, for in my dream I could already hear the lusty roar of the engine and see a young man's lanky dark hair flowing out behind him in the wind.

'He'll bring me flowers,' my sister said.

'And a heart-shaped box of chocolates, made of red velvet with gold round the edges,' I added.

'He'll leap out, and find me, and drive me away to paradise.'

'Hey, but what about me?' I'd thought we did everything together.

'You can have the chocolates,' she said. 'The trouble is, if something real doesn't happen soon, I'm going to be far too old.'

Was she right? As we lay among the daisies, was there a more real life somewhere else? And if so, was it full of grown-up men and passion and art and poetry and music? And was all of it slipping away, out of our reach before we even had time to look for it?

If she said so, it must be true. She was a year and a half older than me.

Our father's cousins liked to call her 'Mariana of the Moated Grange'. It was meant to be a joke. It was a quote from a poet we'd never heard of. The books in our home were either churchy stuff from our mother's side or military history of our father's.

I discovered that the long-dead poet's name was Tennyson and he'd been a lord. I'd have expected our mother to have known about him. She loved lords. And ladies. And royalty. And God. And our father who wert not in heaven but were usually in the same room as her for they had matching writing-desks on either side of the coal fire in their study, and matching beds, side-by-side facing the coal fire in their bedroom. They still seemed very delighted with one another, even after years and years of marriage.

Calling my sister 'Mariana of the Moated Grange' after some old verse, wasn't funny and wasn't true. Yes, okay, so we had moved to live in a huge sprawling house with thirteen bedrooms, four indoor lavatories and one outdoor, but it wasn't a grange, it hadn't got a moat and my sister's name had never been Mariana. It had always been Mary.

'Just like the virgin,' I used to say, which annoyed her a lot. 'All right then,' I'd have to add. 'Like that Scottish queen who had her head chopped off by her sister.'

Mary and I were supposed to be in the fresh bloom of our

youth. I'd overheard one of our mother's friends saying so to another of our mother's friends. Our mother had a lot of friends. Our father didn't seem to have any, possibly because they'd all been killed off in the war, the First World War, that is, not the last one.

'And being youthful is probably why Father's cousins want to make jokes about you,' I said. 'They're jealous of your bloom.'

Mary was tall with long fluffy hair. She wore a pink elastic surgical sock because of her weak ankle that kept spraining. It got her off Games and Gym. I was stout, pink and so short that I had no ankles at all. Or so Mary said. We both had swollen eyes and running itchy noses. It was June. The hayfever season had begun again. The garden was abundant with flowers and pollen-laden grasses.

'I've always known,' Mary said, sitting up and violently blowing her nose, 'that I won't live to be more than twenty-one. So there's very little time left.' Less than a decade. 'If only one just had someone to love.'

'Hm. Anybody would do, I suppose,' I agreed. There was the boy who'd come to help the man who'd been digging over the vegetable patch to get it ready for the broad beans to go in. Tommy had the advantage of being real. But I thought his eyes were so peculiar, and he had such a strong bodily smell that this blocked out the visibility of any of his possible attractions.

'Or even,' Mary said thoughtfully, 'If only one had a baby.'

I sat up abruptly, disturbing the pollen in the grass round

us which set us both sneezing again.

'What on earth for?' I took her handkerchief and blew my nose on a dry corner. I didn't yet know what I *did* want to get out of this section of life but I felt absolutely certain that a baby wasn't it. We had two toddling sisters and a funny younger brother. Wasn't that enough small people to love?

From nearer the house wafted the clink of metal mugs and the merry burble of our parents talking and drinking with other grown-ups. They enjoyed a lot of both.

Mary said, without enthusiasm and without moving, 'Well. Sounds like they're here. Suppose we'll have to get going. She says she needs us there to provide the decorative background. I think it's the Americans. Or the Canadians. Or it might be the BBC again.'

Television crews occasionally came to make programmes about our mother. She wrote verse pageants for holy young people which were said to be very popular, even with the unholy. They were certainly more successful than our father's serious poems and plays on military historical themes, none of which, as far as I knew, had been published or staged during my lifetime.

We could hear our mother calling excitedly for us. Mary rose slowly to her feet, taking care not to put weight on her wobbly left ankle. She shook the grass out of her wafting clouds of hair. It was obvious, even to me, that if any young man happened to be passing down the lane in a sports car, he wouldn't avoid noticing her. He'd immediately skid to a halt and invite her for a spin. They'd fall in love. She'd elope with him and they'd certainly be leaving me behind.

Huh!

But little traffic passed, apart from the milk lorry which hurtled every morning and evening down our lane, to collect the churns from the farms. He was the devil of a driver. I thought he looked a bit like Dirk Bogarde.

Mary said, 'Pah!'

He never slowed to see what lovely maidens might be loitering in the grounds of our home.

As we ambled through the gardens towards the house (which, despite those five lavatories, was definitely no grange because it didn't have a farm attached), our mother saw us through the rose arbour and began sending urgent hurry-up-where-have-you-been-hiding signals with her arms. She was wearing one of her bright floribund frocks especially for the television visitors so she created the vivid impression, against the herbaceous border, of a daytime Catherine wheel.

Mary paused to peer under a rose bush. Her favourite hen, Friendly, was taking a dust-bath.

'Isn't she just so beautiful?' Mary stroked the brown feathers. Couldn't this favourite hen satisfy my sister's yearning for someone to love just as well as a baby might? Friendly eyed us both maliciously, then shuffled deeper into the dirt. Like an Indian cow, the hen had total freedom to wander anywhere in the house or grounds and had never yet been known to produce an egg. Unlike a holy cow, she was able to find her way through the side door, walk upstairs and flap on to the top bunk-beds where she usually left a lot of mites and mess.

There were many bunk-beds for Friendly to choose from because our house was a holiday place for the children of the very rich when their parents wanted to get rid of them for a few weeks, or months, or sometimes even years.

Luckily, the young visitors whose parents paid nine guineas per week for them to holiday here, never minded hen dust. After all, it was supposed to be a *country* holiday. Nor did the local welfare inspector who called to make tri-annual checks just before the Easter hols, the summer hols, and the Christmas hols. She was always far more interested in finding out how our parents managed to combine running their literary lives alongside running the holiday home than in investigating the purity of the beds.

On most visits, the inspector thrust her latest short story on to our father's desk in the hope that he'd find a way of getting it published.

Couldn't she tell from the threadbare elbows of my father's suits that a sensible regular job with the child welfare department of the council was well worth hanging on to? I had actually heard him say, late one night, how the literary life could offer nothing but poverty and pain.

Reluctantly, Mary left Friendly to get on with her toilette and we went to join our parents, our little sisters, the television people and the holiday children on the terrace. Even though it was only early June, they'd already begun gathering like swallows for their long summer holidays. A group clustered eagerly round the cameraman as he began screwing legs on to his tripod. Some of the regular guests were not only the offspring of the rich, but of the richly famous. A few were even slightly famous film-stars themselves so my mother might well have hinted to them that this television visit had been specially laid on for their entertainment.

Friendly completed her bath, hurried down the path to catch up with us, and flapped up into Mary's arms in order to snuggle cosily up under her hair, which might well have seemed to a domesticated hen like a briar thicket.

I wondered if my sister's admirers, when and if any appeared to take her away from all this, would accept a dozen or more furry, feathery, mite-laden companions along with her lovely fluffy-haired self?

TWO

Smile for the Camera

The TV people went on lounging about under the wisteria as though they too were on holiday. They were drinking beer out of our dented silver Christening mugs. The female one, called Denise, with jangling bracelets all up her arms and an imperious voice, seemed to be in charge.

'And so this one is Ruth,' my mother said, pushing me forwards to shake hands.

We were well trained in being polite but I still hated this part, being an exhibit in the family zoo.

'Why, it's all so terribly charming!' shrilled Denise. 'Absolutely enthralling! I've heard *so* much about you, Rebecca.'

'Ruth, actually,' I corrected her.

'Quite so, darling.'

Our parents knew loads of people like her from their previous lives before any of us existed. Not exactly friends, more like long-ago acquaintances they'd once worked with. This one was clearly impressed by the place where our parents had ended up.

'Darlings, it's even more magical than we expected. Oh, *do* look at all that pretty hair they have! *Rousse*, would you say? What fortune to be young, to have such glorious hair! Where *does* it come from?' She glanced eagerly round at our father as though expecting him to recommend the name of a good hair shop.

Just then, Alfred George crawled out of the bushes, and at the sight of his fiery halo of red curls leaping from his little head, Denise's jangling bracelets went into a frenzy of over-excitement.

'Oh, oh, oh!' she cried.

Our brother was named, in keeping with our parents' royalist leanings, after some kings of England. It seemed unfair to me that he'd been given two names while the rest of us only got one.

'It's perfectly obvious why,' Mary had told me firmly. 'He's the boy. So he'll always get more of everything than us.'

Alfred George was wearing a peculiar selection of garments. But then, he always did. He was given a lot of freedom of choice, far too much, in my opinion, for a young boy. Today, he had on a green tartan kilt over a pair of khaki scouting shorts which reached his ankles, with a mighty length of rope coiled round his chest as though he was about to go mountaineering.

'And obviously the spitting image of his papa!' Denise trilled.

She really was a very silly woman. How could someone of

seven in a woollen checked skirt over droopy shorts, wrapped in thick rope, look anything like a tall lean man with a moustache?

'You know what? We simply *must* have interviews with your lovely children too. They're so enchantingly unusual, aren't they, Phil?' Denise nudged one of her dozy colleagues who merely grunted and held out his mug to be re-filled with beer. Or rather, he held out my baby sister Felicity's mug which was what he'd been using. Our parents believed that to enhance the taste of the local draught beer, it must always be drunk from silver.

Denise was enchanted by everything she could see through her dark glasses – the rambling house, the weather, the view across the water meadow (which, if she'd looked more carefully, she might have seen was thick with poisonous floating pollen).

'You know, darlings, you've found true Paradise here. In fact, I'd say it's the South of France, only better! I've *always loathed* the English countryside until today. But then I've never come across such a glorious om–bee–aunts before.'

I thought she must be talking about the wisteria since she was sitting right under it and waving her braceletted arms up at it.

The climbing plant was indeed stunningly beautiful, so much so that sometimes it made me want to cry just looking at it. It was very ancient and the grey trunk clambered up the summerhouse, then under the bedroom windows, pushing its tendrils round the leaded panes. Next, it leaped sideways into mid-air, before catching hold of the silver birch tree growing out of the side of a bank beside the ramparts of the house, and climbing up so that silver birch and wisteria intertwined. Its tender green leaflets fluttered in the breeze and the fallen petals drifted across the flagstones on the terrace like mauve snow.

When Denise started going on about how my parents also had their special om-bee-aunts, which she'd do her best to capture on film, I realised she wasn't talking about wall creepers but about atmosphere. It was her forceful pronounciation of 'ambience', so that it sounded French, that had me confused.

The camera team finally began to drag electric cables out of their van and through the house, trailing them out of doors and windows. The sound engineer wandered round suspending microphones from the branches of the walnut tree. And from the way that Denise kept checking her reflection in a mirror, and taking her dark glasses on and off, it looked like she was finally prepared to start.

'So, first, the establishing long-shot, then zoom in on that baronial door,' she ordered.

'Yeah, loads of ambience in that old wood, along with the death-watch beetle,' muttered Phil, her right-hand man.

Another of the crew began to peer at our parents through a view-finder. Now that I knew that *ambience* was a French word meaning a nice atmosphere, I could see that there was a lot of it about and that our parents had created it. Our father was wearing his battered straw boater, tilted sideways, and using his carved Chinese walking-stick so that it would look as though he didn't really need it except for decoration. His *ambiance* seemed both raffish and distinguished at the same time. Our mother's *ambiance* was more actively ebulliant. She was already slightly flushed with excitement and her hair was springier than usual. Our father once said, after a lunchtime session in the pub with our mother, that he'd married Veritas because she reminded him of a Botticelli cherub.

A cherub of thirty-eight? Parental mutual affection was an odd thing.

So was her name. A lot of people got it wrong and called her Verity, Valerie, Vera or even Fenella. Denise was no exception. Our grandfather was a vicar who'd called each of his daughters after qualities they might aspire to. He'd also decided that each quality must be in a different language. So we had our Aunts Thrift (after the English for being economical), Charité (after the French for charity), and Speranza (after the Italian for hope). Our mother landed up with the Latin word for truth.

'So tell me, Venetia, all these other children, where are they from?'

'Oh, here and there,' my mother said vaguely. 'You know, London, Edinburgh, Borneo, America, Elstree Studios, RADA, Roedean, the Shetland Isles. That sort of thing.'

'And are they all orphans? That would make a nice feature. No, they're not? What a shame. Never mind. Perhaps we could have a shot of them anyway, grouped round your desk looking on, while you're writing?'

I thought, What an absurd idea! Nobody could write with fifteen spare children breathing down her neck. Nor, it quickly transpired, could anyone make a short film about a literary lady with fifteen children hand-standing and grinning like monkeys in front of the camera. Denise was being forced to give up on her story about the life of the writer in favour of one about the children's holiday home, with just a glimpse of the proprietors tacked on at the end.

'You'll both be gazing contentedly through a mullioned window while the little ones gambol outside,' Denise told my parents. 'So now we need all you small folk to sit down here, and make nice daisy-chains. Then, I'll stroll by and you pretend not to notice me. I'll sit down and ask you questions.'

It sounded simple enough but just as Denise was about to start her casual stroll, the arc lamps went out and the camera stopped whirring. The lighting man said, 'Oops, sorry. Overload. Hang on.'

By the time they were ready to re-start, most of the assembled little people had been lured off to take part in a new activity. It was called The Ascent of Everest. It was obviously Alfred George's idea. They were clambering in and out of the bedroom windows using his ropes. The only ones left behind were Felicity and Blanche, my two toddler sisters. Alfred George must have decided they were too small to dangle from his rope. Or perhaps he'd banned them simply because they were his sisters.

It seemed that when our parents named them, they got them the wrong way round for Felicity, far from being felicitous, was a pale solemn baby, whereas Blanche, who ought to have been pale, had screaming red hair, red eyelashes, red eyebrows, and glowing red cheeks and was a bundle of joyful giggles all day long. And camera-crazy with it.

She'd struggled into an enormous satin ballgown out of the dressing-up trunk. She was ready to perform.

Delighted Denise got the camera rolling again. 'So now we come to our very special interview with the proprietors' own five adorable young children,' said Denise into the camera. 'Tell me, dear, why do you like these children coming to stay here for their holidays?' she asked.

Blanche smiled angelically, dimpling her scarlet cheeks and wrinkling her eyes in the phoniest smile a three-year-old could manage. 'I like it 'coth we throwth orange juice,' she lisped.

Denise looked blank. 'Aha,' she said, nodding.

'And we hath fights,' Blanche went on. 'Wid mud. And thtones. Throwing them ath far ath we can. Thometimes we throws them at the big boys, and sometimes the boys throwth them back. Thometimes we just throwth mud. Thometimes we don't throw nothing at all.'

'I see,' said Denise, who obviously didn't. 'So aren't there any rules?'

The brochure, composed by our parents, dreamily described the importance for the developing child of total freedom.

'If you love children enough, they don't need rules,' Veritas used to say.

So there were no rules, except for some dubious ones that

the son of a Hollywood star had invented concerning the playing of Monopoly and a private rule I'd made up that no boy, specially not my brother, should climb the wisteria outside my room and make stupid ghost noises in the night. Nor should any boy borrow Alfred George's ropes and try to lash me to a tree during our exuberant games of cowboys and indians.

'But Ruthie, you know you love it when they do,' Veritas said when I complained.

I wasn't as eager to talk to the camera as Blanche. But if it was good for family business, I was prepared to face the camera and give it a try.

'And next, here's daughter number two in this big happy family,' said Denise pushing the microphone under my nose. 'Tell us, Raquel, just how does it feel to be sharing your family, your home, your parents with all these other kiddies?'

I wasn't to know how much this woman was going to be popping in and out of my future life or I might at least have tried to make sure she got my name right from the very beginning. And what an unfair question to spring on a person! How could I possibly answer truthfully about the bad business of tying me to the trees? How could I answer on the spur of the moment what had been taking me many tense pages in my journal to consider? (And I still hadn't reached a solution).

From the Personal Journal
Trying to think of the GOOD THINGS
Veritas says it's beneficial for my character having to share everything.

(Actually, it often feels very annoying. But if she says so, then it must be OK.)

GOOD: *When we put on plays in the attic.*

GOOD: *having wide range of cast (many with professional experience), musicians, audience.*

GOOD: *having roast potatoes every day for lunch, not just on Sundays.*

GOOD: *going on picnics with six roast chickens.*

GOOD: *playing kick-the-can after dark with enough people to lose a few.*

GOOD: *filling three pews in church on Sunday.*

SOME BAD THINGS:

Just before holidays start, it's panic. Normal family life about to be destroyed. Don't know what to think. But suspect it's probably very BAD. *Want to leave. Run away. Can't. Veritas needs us here to help. Anyway, still too young to leave home. Can't drive. Can't afford it on 6$^{d.}$ a week pocket money. (Not enough to get far enough.)*

BAD: *Must be very unworthy person* BUT *do* NOT *like lending books, clothes.* DO NOT *like moving out of bedroom for juvenile film-stars.* DO NOT *like sharing use of home and parents.*

MORE BAD: *Do not like continual embarrassment of 6$^{d.}$ pocket money when most visitors get sent ten shillings per week from their parents.*

These important thoughts were from before the big hols started. But while the holidays were actually happening, there was less time for stopping and thinking about feelings. And then, as the end of each holiday approached, there was a new dread. How would one bear the emptiness when we were back to being a small family of only seven, when half the bedrooms were empty, except for Friendly scrabbling like a winged ghost from bed to bed.

Denise was fidgeting impatiently with the mike.

'Er yes,' I began. 'This is a very important issue. I think it feels like—'

But I'd taken too long. My three seconds of fame had slipped by, unused. 'No? Ahh, it looks like Ruth is too shy to voice an opinion.'

Denise turned her back on me, beamed into the camera and was about to round off her interview when Cook came steaming past like a squat dwarf in her white overalls and cap, and the shot was spoiled. 'First she tells me lunch for nineteen! Ten minutes later it's lunch for thirty-five. And now just look at the clock! We haven't even sat down and before we know where we are, it'll be time for tea.'

What was really upsetting her was the lighting assistant who'd moved into the kitchen and was preparing to illuminate the roast beef and green beans. 'Him and his lamps! Killing off the vitamins. My meals are for eating, not for being filmed. Next thing, they'll be melting the crumble and cream with that heat.'

Cook stomped back indoors before my parents even had time to calm her down with the usual soothing words. Cook had a tantrum at least once a day though never threatened to hand in her notice and leave. She couldn't afford to. The other place where she lived during term-times, was in a boys' preparatory boarding school. She was assistant cook. Of all the scary things that might happen to a person, having no real home of their own seemed to me to be the worst. Cook had a silent daughter of Alfred George's age. My home was the nearest Pauline ever got to a real one. If I minded about having to share so much of my life, I knew I was unworthy. Poor Pauline didn't even have a bedroom of her own, let alone a father to share.

When the lights were switched off and the camera stopped whirring, Denise asked my parents, 'Don't you ever have accidents here?'

She'd noticed that the gang of boys, having completed several successful descents from the windows, had armed themselves with gardening tools from the potting shed and were drifting towards the meadow.

'We've got to dig some tunnels,' Alfred George called. 'We're going to re-enact the Escape from Colditz.'

'Yes, of course,' said Veritas proudly. 'Simply loads. The people in Emergency at the Cottage Hospital are old friends. There's scars and stitches on most of them. All inflicted here.'

Denise's mouth gaped. 'Don't parents sue?'

'Goodness no,' said Veritas. 'That's why they send their children here. For the freedom, for the marvellous exposure to danger we offer.'

'They have to pay extra if their children are wounded,' said my father with a charming smile which showed his flash of gold tooth. A long, long time ago, in the days of silent movies, before any of us had been born, he'd been a film-star. You still couldn't tell when he was telling the truth and when he was acting.

These days, filming offered no starring roles, except for Denise, and certainly no freedoms or dangers.

Cook stomped back to the kitchen.

Felicity and Blanche toddled up the garden path, accompanied by two little girls from the Royal Ballet School, as dainty as fairies, and poor silent plodding Pauline. They were on their way to sit inside the fruit cage and feast on unripe strawberries straight from the plant. Marie-Claire from Paris who used her six weeks' freedom here to stay in bed as long as possible, hurried past the window towards the pantry to make herself a dozen pieces of toast. She'd discovered that true freedom was to be able to stay in bed all day and eat nothing but white sliced bread.

Mary and I went to lie on a different lawn, under a different tree, this time towards the front of the house. Then, if by some miracle something of interest should happen on the quiet lane beyond, we would not miss it.

We were in luck.

No sooner had we settled ourselves beneath the billowing pear blossom, than we heard a hopeful scrunching on the drive, followed by a clanking rattle, and a timid throat-clearing.

'I think it's a man on a bicycle,' I whispered. Well, more of a young lad really. 'D'you suppose he's come to see us?'

THREE

An Admirer on the Horizon

The driveway was completely jammed with the television peoples' cars and vans. From behind our screen of gently waving grasses, we watched as he dismounted. Carefully, he took off his cycle clips. From this distance, he looked quite male, even if not as darkly devilish as the milk lorry driver.

As he turned and wondered where he could safely leave his bike, Mary and I recognised Timmy. He had a lock of sandy hair which kept falling over his face, and soft pink neck and ears. But he was definitely better than nothing. He was the cub reporter from the *Weekly Express and County Tribune*. At the pony club gymkhana he could be seen cowering beside high jumps waiting for girls to take a fall so that he could write a paragraph about it. At the flower show he hovered outside the big marquee ready to creep up on the embroidered traycloth winner. It was obvious he hadn't come to see us. He must have come to see Veritas. Whenever the paper was short of news, they'd send someone out to check on what she was up to.

We saw him lie his bike down gently beside the blue hydrangeas, take a spiral-bound shorthand notepad out of his saddle-bag, then sidle cautiously, like one of Mary's more nervous fowl, towards the front door. It was wide open. Denise was having some brilliant new ideas about gathering everybody together, piling them into our van, driving them to the coast and filming them bathing in the sea.

'They won't all fit into the van,' Veritas was saying. 'We'd have to do it in two journeys. By the time we'd got the second load down to the beach, the first lot would've finished swimming and be starving hungry and ready to come home.'

'I'd really love to get the ambience of the seaside in,' said Denise.

Timmy stood patiently at our mother's elbow, waiting for his turn to speak. He had his notepad open in his hand. He coughed politely. Veritas seemed to think he was asking when the next meal would be. She waved him away.

'Go and ask Mary or Ruth, there's a dear,' she said.

'B-b-but you p-p-p-promised me!' he said. Timmy had a terrible stutter.

'I can't have. I never make promises. And can't you see I'm busy just now? But if you really can't wait, why not have a banana? Or find something nice in the larder. There's lots of trifle. Or what about a hundreds-and-thousands sandwich?'

Among the non-rules of freedom at our parents' establishment was one that implied any child-guest may help themselves to any food they felt like at any time of day or night. Cook found it very irritating.

'There's none of this please-yourself nonsense going on at my prep school,' she growled.

Veritas dismissed Timmy and he darted back to hover by the security of his bike.

'I feel a bit sorry for him, don't you?' said Mary in the same way that she said she'd felt sorry for the cockerel when he'd been pecked by Friendly and the other hens. She sat up.

'Can we help you?' she said.

I sat up too and tried to look more alluring than a schoolgirl with bad hay fever.

'Oh! H-h-h-hello,' said Timmy. 'I r-r-rang the or-or-or-author only yesterday. She p-p-p-promised to give me an interview. Now she w-w-won't speak to me. I d-d-don't know what I'll tell my editor if I go back without even a picture.'

Mary suggested, 'Couldn't you take a picture of us instead?'

'It's s-s-supposed to be a f-f-feature about the au-au-author's latest venture.'

'It still could be. Only with a picture of us instead of her.'

'V-v-very well,' said Timmy, blinking uncertainly.

So we posed, Mary decoratively against the pear tree while I swung fetchingly upside down from a branch just above her head.

Timmy clicked the shutter of his camera just once before putting it back in his saddle-bag. The press reporters who'd come to see our mother from London papers usually made a whole roll of exposures. But I didn't tell Timmy.

He said, 'S-s-so what's the story?'

I said, 'I think it's just the same old stuff she always writes.

You know, about the Girl Guides doing good turns, and humanity and God, and doing your bit for the world. And I think there may be some royalty thrown in this time.'

'N-n-n-no. B-b-b. I-I-I-I,' Timmy spluttered.

Mary said, 'I don't think he means *her* story. He means what shall he write under the piccy.'

He nodded and licked the end of his pencil in readiness to take down whatever we thought up for him. Unlike Denise who was chockfull of ideas, Timmy seemed to have none of his own. He only knew that he had to get his two hundred words back to the editor on time.

'What about "Contentment is book-shaped"?' I suggested. Timmy didn't think much of that.

'Well, what about "Local author's new work is so good you'll want to read about it upside down"? That'd be good with a picture of me swinging. And then you give all the details about where it's being put on and how much it costs to get in. Or how about a rhyming couplet? That'd be unusual. "See these sisters! What do they say? They're publicising their mother's play."'

Timmy said he didn't think his editor was modern enough for my ideas. In the end he wrote, with Mary's help, "Two sisters, Mary and Ruth, were today seen jumping for joy over their authoress mother's latest oeuvre."

I said, 'But we weren't jumping. Mary was leaning and I was swinging and you've made it sound as though we're actually jumping over the pageant.'

Timmy didn't seem to think it mattered. He put on his

cycle clips and pedalled off looking very pink and happy.

Much later that evening, when tea was over, and high tea and supper, and the last game of Monopoly had been played, just as I was feeding the cats in the yard, I heard a breathy whistling through the yew tree. It definitely wasn't the barn owl, though it didn't scare me because it could easily have been the breathless old badger that shuffled about in the lane. Or most likely one of the hedgehogs that liked to come and eat the expensive Kit-e-Kat I spooned out into saucers and left on the ground.

I was about to go indoors to let hedgehogs and cats sort it out for themselves when the whistler called my name.

'R–R–R–Ruth.'

Timmy was back. Or perhaps he'd never really gone away.

'Y–y–y–you're at the grammar school, aren't you?'

'So?'

'I–I–I–I've s–s–s–seen you playing hockey.'

He can't have been telling the truth. Nobody ever saw me play hockey. I avoided it by any means possible. On the two occasions I'd been forced on to the pitch, I opted for the shelter of goal where the only danger of being involved in the game was if the ball came too near and hurt your shins.

'Maybe,' I said, for he might have mistaken me for one of the other players. From a distance, we must all have looked like navy blue blobs.

'C–c–can I meet you one day?'

'When?'

'N–n–next week? A–a–a–after school?'

Good idea, I thought. Then he could push my bike up the steep hills. But I said, 'What for?'

'W-w-we could t-t-t-talk.'

I had a sudden image of other girls giggling behind their hands when they saw how soft and pink Timmy's ears were, rather like Mary's pet mice.

'No, I don't think so. The teachers don't like people hanging round the gate.' The boys' grammar school was built right next to ours, but we were kept strictly segregated. Even on the school buses, a sturdy member of staff kept pupils separate, boys on top, girls underneath.

'Th-th-th-th-th-th-then?' Whatever it was he wanted to say next was so urgent it took ages to get it out. 'Then, d'you want to come for a walk with me now, down the lane?'

A stroll in the gloaming? That was the sort of thing Mariana of the Moated Grange got up to. Timmy's eagerness took me by surprise.

I saw my father and Veritas sitting side by side on their matching deck-chairs, while various small children romped about like so many happy bunnies in the rosy glow of the evening sun. At first, I couldn't take in what Timmy was trying to say. When I did, I was suddenly terrified out of my wits. How could I possibly venture out of the garden with him? What if he tried to hold my hand, or kiss me, or put his arm round my shoulder? I'd die of embarrassment. And I felt I could hear my mother's mocking laughter. *Ruthie's gone for a walk down the lane with that cub reporter from the paper! Tee hee hee! What a scamp she is.*

'I should think not!' I said huffily. 'Why should I want to go off for a walk with you?'

Timmy's ears went very pink. He blinked hard and twitched his nose like a frightened rabbit.

'I'm perfectly all right here in the garden, thank you,' I went on, more firmly than I meant. But why ever did I say that I was all right? Of course I wanted to go with him.

If only Timmy had insisted, just once. But he didn't. He scrambled back on to his bike and pushed off up the hill. When Mary heard I'd turned down my first date, she said I was daft. 'Course you should've gone. I'd have. He might've walked you all the way to the seaside, taken you to the soda fountain and bought you a lime fizz.'

I said, 'When I get taken somewhere, I don't want to be *walked*. I want to be *driven*, in a proper sports car. And for the time being, I think things are fine just as they are.'

'I'd do anything to get away.'

But why should we want to leave our happy Paradise with its goats and cats, dogs and bikes, gardens and copious meals, its warmth and comfort and company? Why should we ever want anything to change?

I wasn't to know, nor was Mary, that this heavenly existence wouldn't last much longer. But even if I *had* known what horrors lurked ahead, there was nothing I could have done to stop them happening.

FOUR

Grim Reaping

Mary said she always knew. But how could she possibly tell?

He had it in his eyes, so she claimed.

'He has what?'

'The look of death.'

'You sure?'

'Yes. Animals get it too, when they know their time's up. Remember my goat we had to have put down?' Hard to forget Mr Billy with the mighty strength of an ox, and the curving horns, hard as steel, who broke free from his tether to chase Alfred George across the orchard, who nibbled the tops off the sprouting greens, and the washing hanging on the line, who butted a moving van denting its mudguards, before making off down the lane in search of a mate and a better life.

'He knew, even before the knacker's man got here with the truck. That's why he went so quietly.'

But it wasn't just Mary's favourite goat. During the next thirteen busy months, the man with the long scythe was up and down our country lanes and by-ways, lopping off the young and the old, the tall and the short, the feathered and the pink-skinned.

Grandfather was the first to go, not so much struck down by the reaper as lifted up by the angels. As he had sown, so most certainly would he reap. Grandfather sowed words of joy for this life and for life everlasting in the next. He was rector of the parish two villages distant, an hour's bike ride, half an hour in the bus. These days, he was so old that he peed in a potty which he kept under a pew or hid beneath the black skirts of his cassock. His hair was already as white as the clouds in the sky. He refused to obey his bishop and retire. He died instead.

When Veritas told us, I felt sad, but not unbearably so. Mary didn't cry at all and I only a very little. For the magnificent funeral, we both got the afternoon off school. Veritas had her hair done and our father looked discreetly distinguished in a black tailcoat and pinstripe trousers which, unlike most of his suits, seemed scarcely worn at all. It was quite a different look from the raffish boater.

'Where does it come from?' I asked Veritas.

'Out of his wardrobe of course. Father always wears his morning suit for funerals,' she said, as though I ought to know.

'Well I've never seen him wear it before,' I said.

'That's because he hasn't needed to get it out since King George's do in Westminster Abbey.'

I was meant to remember about that too. The newspaper headlines, 'THE KING IS DEAD' and 'WHEN A NATION MOURNS' had been memorable. So had the three queens,

Mary, Elizabeth and Elizabeth, so heavily veiled in black they looked like beekeepers.

For Grandfather, the flowers and wreaths were so many that they flowed out of the church and, when they were lined up on either side of the path, they stretched right down to the lych-gate. The scent was as rich as a summer's day and made you feel you were almost in heaven already.

Hundreds came, every soul from the parish, and more mourners from the far corners of the county. Friends, relations, descendants, filled every pew, even the dusty ones at the back. They were being crammed into the side-chapels, standing in the porch, and still crowding round the west door so that it was quite a squeeze for the six Sidesmen to stagger in with the coffin.

He liked a full house.

'Rector'd be pleased at the turnout,' observed one of the church wardens who was ushering.

Would have been pleased? Surely, he was pleased. From his seat in heaven, he could see everything that was going on.

Our mother's brothers, the scary uncles, Falcon, Merlin and Kestrel, were here. Grandfather had named them after meat-eating birds of prey. Only the youngest, Uncle Guillemot, was a sea-bird. He was also a vicar and emerged from the vestment room with a bevvy of ordained men, and they shuffled to form into an orderly procession. Our aunts, Thrift, Charité, and Speranza were here too, together with their numerous offspring. I hoped that some of these cousins would notice how fine my father looked in a suit that had experienced the funeral of a king. But perhaps they had eyes only for the naval, military and priestly outfits of their own fathers.

'So that'll be all twenty-seven of the reverend's grandchildren brought along to see him off,' one of the church wardens whispered loudly and approvingly to another.

Twenty-seven was not counting the stillborn, the miscarried and the two who didn't survive their first year of life, but had gone ahead to be ready and waiting with Saint Peter to welcome Grandfather in through those golden gates.

Our grandmother walked to her pew straight-backed, silent, but not distraught like those three veiled beekeeper queens. She sat directly beneath the pulpit from which Grandfather had been preaching for the past thirty-five years. Now he lay in the aisle right beside her, so close she could reach out and touch the coffin with her gloved hand.

As the first part of the service ended, and it was time for her to leave her pew and follow the coffin outside for burial, our grandmother raised her hand imperceptibly towards me, beckoning me to join her in that important place right behind the body. The crowds parted to let us through. The choir sang.

Some people stared as we passed down the church, some wept, some smiled. Some might even have been praying. My grandmother took my hand lightly in hers, though didn't look at me. I felt smaller than usual, but so proud. Of the twenty-seven, she had chosen me.

I caught the glare of my cousins Faith and Petra. They were looking daggers. Why *you*? they seemed to be asking. Why does our Granny ask you to walk with her?

Because I am her favourite. Because I am named after her. But I knew that my privileged place in Granny's affection could never be flaunted.

After we'd seen him lowered into the deep hole and flowers thrown in, the multitudes drove or were driven, or walked, or rode, or biked or ran directly over the fields, the two miles to the rectory for tea and egg sandwiches and little cakes with crystallised violets on top. And again, there was not room for all the mourners to fit in, so they spilled out of our grandmother's drawing room and into the hall and out of the front door and down the steps into the garden.

Oh, what a way to go! If this was the aftermath of death, what was there to fear?

When we reached home, there was a flamboyant bouquet of waxy white lilies waiting in the main hall. They'd been delivered all the way from a florist in Mayfair. I knew Mayfair well from the Monopoly board. It was the poshest bit of London.

'Who on earth can they be from?' said Veritas.

Tucked into the cellophane was a black-edged, candle-decorated card, with an extravagant message of condolence.

'From your television friend?' suggested my father.

'*My* friend?' said Veritas.

'Well, wasn't she?' he said.

Veritas put the lilies in a jug of water. But my father said, did she really want to make the hall look like a B-movie Chapel of Rest? and anyway the smell was making him wheeze. So Veritas put them outside.

I liked B-movies. I thought the lilies were lovely. I went out and read the card.

'*Darling Darlings! Saw about your tragic loss in* The Times. *Thinking of you deeply during these dark days. As ever, Denise.*'

Aha! So it *was* from that bossy woman who'd come with the television crew in the summer. But why should she think Grandfather's death was tragic? He was eighty-five, more than five times as old as Mary was now, and over four times older than she was intending to live. And what, moreover, were dark days? Today had been wonderful. I'd really enjoyed it. Just as well I'd made the most of it for the rest of the dyings weren't half as much fun.

The week after Grandfather's funeral, Mary's puppy escaped from her kennel and killed two of the next-door farmer's hens. He threatened to shoot her on sight if it happened again. So the dog had to be chained up with one of the decaying corpses (she'd eaten the other one) attached to her collar to remind her, night and day, of the wages of dog sin. This, according to the local mole-catcher, who also knew about dog training, was the only sure way of training a killer dog not to re-offend. The smell was terrible.

No sooner had the dog been cured of her hen-chasing tendencies than Fowl Pest came sweeping across the countryside, ruining farmers' lives, not to mention the lives of their infected chickens. Our hamlet had two mixed farms, the Goldfinches at the top of the hill, two of whose hens had already met their end in the jaws of Mary's puppy, and the Hares at the bottom. Both farmed chickens and dairy cattle.

There was only one cure for Fowl Pest. Incineration. The order from the Ministry of Agriculture came and the smell of burning sinews and feathers filled the air, seeped round the closed windows into our homes. It crept up our nostrils as we cycled to school even though we wound our striped scarves tightly round our faces, like Touaregs keeping out the desert sand.

Hundreds of carcasses had to be pitch-forked up on to the burning pyres. The farmers and their wives and their labourers were glum. Timmy turned up on his bike to interview them as they watched the mass cremation of their hens.

'M-M-M-Mrs Goldfinch, w-w-w-what does it feel like to stand here and s-s-s-see this f-f-f-fire b-b-b-burn?'

The week before the *Weekly Express and County Tribune* had carried a snappy news item called *Killer Dog Disaster Alarms Many Farmers*. It had looked like Timmy's work. It had been a gross misrepresentation of the true facts about one over-excited puppy and two hens. Mary suspected Timmy had been fed his information by the mole-catcher. At least with the Fowl Pest story, Timmy had a genuinely disastrous subject to inspire him.

In order to contain the disease, every poultry bird had to go. Friendly, and her egg-laying pals were looking so sprightly as they strutted around the flower-beds. Even the hen-pecked cockerel was looking proud and cheerful now his plumage had re-grown.

'They've never been near any of the Goldfinches' stock,' said Mary sadly.

But they had to have their necks wrung and be tossed on to a bonfire in the garden.

Next, one of my dearest young cats was run over by the milk lorry as it hurtled on its rounds. The body was hundreds of yards away down the lane. What was my kitty doing roaming so far from home, so early in the morning?

'She must have had the urge to travel,' said Mary. 'Perhaps she just felt it was time to leave home?'

The fiendish driver didn't even stop.

Alfred George said, 'Probably he didn't notice the bump as he went over her.'

More likely he wanted to get the milk collected before it curdled in the churns.

Timmy did not consider this single cat death important enough to be worth investigating for a newspaper report. So it was Tommy, the boy who dug the garden, who scraped up my cat's flattened remains on a shovel, carried her up the lane, and dug me a hole beyond the sprouting broccoli. After she was buried, I heaved up a large paving slab from one of the paths in the garden to use as a head-stone. I started to carve a suitable inscription.

In Memoriam. Here lies a Dearly Beloved Cat and Companion. Born March 1955 Died May 1955 it was going to say. But chiselling out York stone with a screw-driver was far harder work than I expected so after a whole Saturday's chiselling, the memorial stone read only, *In Me.* That would have to do.

Tommy set it in place and read it several times over with his lips moving, then plucked up courage to ask, 'What's that mean?'

'It's Latin,' I said. 'It sort of means, "Rest in Peace".'

'Ah, that's nice,' he said and looked as me with respect and admiration for being so clever knowing the Latin. I felt bad for minding his smell and his protruding eyes and for cheating him by pretending to be cleverer than he was and cleverer than I was.

The next bereavement was multiple. One of Mary's pet mice, (though luckily not her favourite) unexpectedly gave birth to a litter of five. The male gobbled them up within hours of delivery.

Blanche and Felicity, who'd seen the tiny pink slug-like newborns before they were consumed by their father, were impressed rather than upset. But Alfred George was a know-all.

'You knew that might happen!' he said. 'You should've separated them.'

'I was going to,' Mary said. 'But how was I to know she'd go into labour while I was at school?'

Once the Fowl Pest was declared by the Ministry of Agriculture to be well and truly gone, Mary re-stocked her henhouse with guinea fowl and Muscovy ducks. The Goldfinches too, re-stocked, though not with free-range poultry again. They went modern and brought in battery farming. These hens were housed in sheds and never saw the light of day.

Country life was harsh. The two farms just about seemed to be pulling themselves together when a new scourge turned up.

'They call it Foot and Mouth Disease,' Mary told me, adjusting the pink elastic sock on her ankle. 'Cows get it.'

This time, not just the county, but dairy farms all over the country were affected. Both the Goldfinch and Hare farms were in quarantine, which meant that our hamlet was sealed off to through-traffic. Only essential vehicles bringing farm supplies had access. Moving livestock or horses was banned too, so the foxhounds were no longer allowed to exercise in their cheerful yelping pack but had to be kept in their kennel yard in the village.

One morning Mary and I discovered barriers set up across the lane, together with shallow concrete troughs, filled with disinfectant.

'So now we can't possibly get to school,' Mary announced with delight, starting to turn back.

But a health inspector came by and explained that we had to dismount from our bikes and wheel them through the purifying troughs.

'It'll take ages if we have to get off every time we reach a trough,' I said.

'Why don't we try speeding up instead?' Mary suggested.

So we got up speed and pedalled furiously over the bumps and right through the milky liquid which splashed up and saturated our gymslips. The stink lingered all day and discouraged other girls from wanting to sit near us, let alone be our partners in gymastics.

Any girls who, like us, came in from rural areas, were anyway considered to be oikish and dim. Now we were shunned like lepers. The Biology teacher made an unconvincing announcement in Morning Assembly that Foot and Mouth Disease was not transmittable to humans. But it made little difference. Girls still yelled, 'Watch out, here comes Big Foot and Little Mouth,' when they saw us pedalling towards the bike-sheds.

Timmy was keeping well away too.

FIVE

God Bless the Master of this House

In the mornings, it was still murky when we set out. In the afternoons, dusk was already gathering before we got back, so all our decent daylight hours were used up in school.

'Such a waste,' Mary said.

Arriving home out of the half-dark, with only two weeks to go till Christmas, we found something curious. Our father was in bed. He'd been there all day. How odd, when he hated wasting time in bed. He said that the dust in the blankets made his asthma worse.

'Father was just feeling a bit tired,' Veritas said vaguely. 'Go up and see him. Tell him I'm bringing the tea in a moment.'

He was sitting up wearing a pair of spectacles as well as the monocle which he kept on a black silk string round his neck, now tucked below the ridge of his right eyebrow. He didn't look tired. He looked busy and comfortable.

One dog, two cats, Blanche, Felicity, a typewriter, and a half-written manuscript were on the bed around him. A couple of empty Christening mugs lay on the floor, suggesting that his lunch with Veritas had been pleasantly sociable with beer. The coal fire burned brightly in the grate. Fortunate father, not having to slog off to dreary school all day.

The only uncomfortable aspect of the room was his bed. The foot-end was propped up on an empty beer barrel so that it was higher than the pillow-end. Despite the steep slope, our father was maintaining a dignified semi-upright position.

'Hello,' I said. 'Why's the bed like this?'

'Your sweet mother's idea,' he said with a smile, as though he'd put up with anything that amused her.

'But what for?'

'Coth he'th draining hith lungs,' said Blanche. 'The thilly doctor says. So's they'll get better.'

What did a four-year-old know about draining wet lungs?

He was doing *The Times* crossword puzzle. 'That looks difficult,' I said.

'No, not really. As a matter of fact, it's somewhat akin to knitting,' he said. 'Only not as noisy.' He didn't like loud noises which must have sometimes made life with five children hazardous. Mary said it was something to do with the bombs in the First World War.

Veritas arrived with the tray of currant buns and tea. But it wasn't a good idea. The company of children sitting quietly on his bed, of cats and dogs silently lapping milk out of saucers on the floor, of Veritas stoking up the fire, was more exhausting than it might seem. Even the sounds of people eating buns began to distress him. He started to wheeze, then to gasp desperately for breath. He had drugs for his asthma. They didn't seem to be working as well as usual.

'D'you suppose, my darling,' Veritas said when the attack was beginning to pass, 'that maybe I should put off the holiday children before it's too late?'

The first batch of them were due to arrive the next day. It was already far too late for any such puttings-off.

Veritas said, 'Just till we see how you are?'

'Of-course-not, my-sweet,' my father said, patting her hand. He spoke slowly because speaking and breathing simultaneously was quite difficult for him. 'Where-else-would-the-little-dears-go? I'll-just-keep-out-of-draughts-and-try-not-to-breathe-on-them.'

'It's not you breathing on them I'm worried about! It's them breathing on you, with all their little boarding school sniffles.'

As usual, as planned, the children arrived anyway with their trunks full of dirty uniform, and their large amounts of pocket money, and they settled themselves easily into my home as their home. It felt extra lousy having to go to school through the drizzle when they were already in relaxed mood, happily stringing up Christmas cards and making tree decorations with Veritas, helping ice the cakes and bake the mince-pies with Cook.

Meanwhile, despite keeping out of draughts, despite the beer barrel under the end of his bed, despite daily sociable visits from the doctor, who always stayed for a friendly mug of draught bitter, our father wasn't getting better.

I was contentedly doodling French *làlàlà*'s down the white

margins of *Mariette et Paul à la campagne* in my first lesson of the day, with ten minutes to go before the end-of-session bell when the school secretary bustled into the classroom. Mariette and Paul's promenade along the riverbank had to be halted when the secretary called out my name.

'Your mother says she wants you,' she said sternly. 'She phoned from the hospital. Your sister's in the cloakroom. She's waiting for you. So hurry along now.'

Mary was lurking in the shadows by the stacked-up milk crates. At the sight of her with her beret pulled on, her gaberdine already belted and buckled, my eyes unaccountably filled with tears which blurred the world. I had to grope my way along the rows of macs and shoe-bags to find my own peg. As I struggled to get my arms into the sleeves, the wetness brimmed over and bounced down my front.

'Not now,' Mary hissed. 'Everybody will see. At least wait till we're outside.'

I didn't even know yet what I was crying about. But I knew she was right. The moment the bell went, the cloakroom would become a heaving crossroads of humanity who gawped and stared at anything out of the ordinary, like hot tears before ten o'clock.

The Latin mistress drove us to the hospital, dumped us at the entrance, and spluttered away as fast as her little Austin 7 would carry her. There was nobody to tell us where to go, what to do next. We wandered along shiny empty corridors. Eventually we found the ward full of men.

'Oh good! I thought you'd want to be here,' Veritas

greeted us, as though to an important theatrical performance. 'I knew you wouldn't want to feel left out!'

Our father was behind a pretty floral curtain. They'd put him in a white metal cot like a big baby because he was delirious and thrashing about.

'Yes, I knew you'd want to come,' Veritas kept saying, flinging her arms out in wide expansive gestures.

Why? We couldn't speak to him. He was unconscious. We couldn't do anything helpful because we were only children. It was horrible. I didn't want to be there. I'd been summoned. The nurses bustled about. We were definitely in the way.

'I think we'd better go now,' Mary said quietly, tugging my arm.

'Are you sure?' Veritas said uncertainly, as though she didn't want to be left on her own with this stranger. 'Very well. Perhaps you had.' Had she realised it was pointless to have three of us squeezed in behind the curtain? 'Oh but you can't go! You haven't got your bikes.' She fished in her purse and gave us a two-shilling piece. Four weeks' pocket money! Had she lost her reason? 'You'd better take a bus.'

It was a nice idea but she must have gone a bit off her rocker because no buses went within two miles of our hamlet.

Like the Latin mistress fifteen minutes earlier, Mary and I couldn't escape from the hospital quick enough. Outside, it was still drizzling and there seemed nowhere obvious for us to go. We trailed aimlessly along the main road towards the sea. Mary abruptly veered off the pavement as though she couldn't walk in a straight line any more, and began to scramble up the steep and muddy bank alongside the road. On it grew spindly elm trees swagged with ivy. So I followed. We reached the top. We could see people and cars passing below but nobody could see us. The trees made us feel safe. We stood for an hour, not moving, not speaking for there was nothing to say, not crying, just standing as the rain dripped through the branches on to our berets and the mud seeped into our lace-ups. Under the circumstances, it felt like the only thing to do.

I wish she hadn't made us go, I thought of saying, but then knew that it didn't need to be said out loud.

Eventually, we slid down the slope and started for home. Mary stopped at a newsagent on the edge of town to spend the largesse from Veritas's purse.

'I'll get something for the little ones, shall I?' she said. 'To cheer them up.'

I waited outside the shop. My lips felt wobbly as though they wouldn't work. She came out with three chocolate decorations, festive in silver wrappers with gold thread for tying them to the tree. She'd chosen a Christmas dog, a Christmas clock and a Christmas car.

We plodded through the suburbs. When we were out in the country, the egg delivery van stopped to offer us a lift.

'Playing truant then, lassies?' the eggman asked with a knowing wink.

We both nodded. Easier than trying to explain. And we didn't even know yet what there was to explain.

Blanche and Felicity didn't seem in any special need of

cheering up. But then they hadn't seen our father thrashing about. Alfred George was inventing a new game with some of the boys up in the attic. All three were pleased with their chocolate novelties. Felicity asked if she should break her Christmas car into enough pieces to share with every child in the house.

I said, 'Well, they're really meant for hanging on the tree till Christmas.'

'That's right,' agreed Alfred George. 'You're supposed to wait till they've gone a bit mouldy before you eat them. It's traditional.'

'But I *like* my clock! I don't want it mouldy,' said Blanche. 'I'm going to eat it now.'

Mary and I had missed dinner at school. We'd missed it at home too. Cook made us each a boiled egg with toast fingers as though we were ill. She draped our coats on the front rail of the Aga.

'You'll catch your deaths with them wet clothes on,' she scolded, then immediately looked as though she wished she hadn't. 'I mean, I'm sure you don't have to be going back to school if you don't want to, not with them damp things. They'll understand. And if they don't, then they're acting criminal.'

I said, 'But I *want* to! There's double Chemistry this afternoon.' It wasn't the Chemistry I needed. It was the escape from this horrible confusing day back into the security of dull normality.

I grabbed a spare bike from the barn. It was one I'd long

since outgrown and so had Alfred George. It had no gears and small wheels. I peddled hard and reached school just in time for the afternoon classes. It was another big mistake.

Life was no more normal in the Chemistry lab than it had been anywhere else. The work benches, the tripods, the gas taps, all had a distant unreal appearance. I was reprimanded for not paying attention with the test tubes. Tears welled up.

I pretended it was from escaping ammonia.

I wanted to ask if I could leave the room. But I didn't know how to explain it. What were the right words for describing what I had seen in a hospital cot this morning? And even if I did find the right words, once I said them the event might become true, whereas if I said nothing the memory could fade away.

I fiddled with the test-tubes in their wooden stands, stirred things with the glass rod, not knowing what experiment we were supposed to be doing. Suddenly, further down the bench, a girl set fire to another girl's plait with the Bunsen burner. It was quite deliberate and the plait was so long that the victim didn't realise for some moments that she was on fire. But the smell of melting hair soon caught the teacher's attention. She became hoarse with hysterical rage. Every pupil along the bench, including the girl with the shrivelled and shortened plait, was accused of irresponsible behaviour. The navy blue satin ribbon on the end of the plait had burned too.

Chemical experimention had resumed when the headmistress's silhouette appeared like a black bat in the glass door. She always wore the gown awarded her by some university to remind us how clever she was. It was rumoured that she even wore it at home. Usually she had cleverer things to do than go round tracing the smell of burning hair.

For the second time that day, my name was called and I was ordered out of class. It was very shaming.

I shuffled into the corridor, head hanging. Is this it? Has something truly and irreversibly bad now happened? Should I feel grief-stricken? Or should I feel guilty?

Guilt won. I felt unaccountably responsible for the hair-burning incident. I loathed Muriel Pogle. She loathed me. It could so easily have been me that did it. Perhaps, in a moment of wilfulness, I had, and amnesia had instantly blotted it from my memory.

The headmistress glared down at me with eyes like screw-in cup hooks. She tapped me firmly on the shoulder so that the sleeve of her grand gown flapped like a big wing. She was not a bat but a black angel.

'Now then,' she said. What did she mean? 'Now then Rebecca, you're perfectly old enough to know what is going on, are you not?'

Was I? I had no idea how old you had to be.

'So from now on, you're going to have to try and be very very good. Do you understand what I mean?'

I bit my lip. I tried to nod. But I knew that I didn't understand anything. Even the experiment in the lab with all those little crystals that melted made more sense to me than this cryptic conversation.

'So very well. Now run along back to your class like a

sensible girl. I've expected good things of you.'

After that, there was no possibility of asking permission to go home early. If only one could be tucked up in bed with a jolly adventure book, a fire flickering in the grate and soup on a tray.

Without Mary, it was a lonely ride home. The battery in the front lamp was giving out. Its light was dim and flickery, more like a candle. To save power, I switched it off for the uphill walks. As I was pushing up the last steep hill in near-dark, a panting figure caught up with me. It was Tommy Groundsel returning from one of his farmhand jobs. Like his father, his brothers, and his uncle, he was a casual labourer so he was a lot worse off than me. He didn't even have a too-small bike to ride on. Nor did his dad. Nor any of his family. They walked wherever they had to get to. They lived in a single-storey cabin with a small plot of land and an outdoor privy. Tommy probably didn't have a bedroom of his own.

'Afternoon,' he muttered.

'Hm-hm,' I replied.

I wasn't sure if I was crying but I thought I might be so I didn't want to speak too much.

He said, 'You sound a bit rough. What's up?'

'Chilblains,' I croaked.

It was true that my hands were so cold they were practically sticking to the handlebars. But chilblains wasn't true. Even if they had been, they were not worth weeping over.

'Sorry,' he said.

He'd been so nice about my dead cat. I hated lying to him.

I said, 'Gloves got wet this morning.' At least that part was true.

I could tell he'd have liked to take one of my hands and warm it in his. Please please please, I begged silently, don't let him touch me, not even my hand, not even by mistake.

Tommy was a boy labourer. I was a girl who knew Latin. He was so respectful he didn't even offer to help me push my bike. We reached the crest of the hill. Time for me to remount and rush away from him, downhill with hot wet in the eyes and cold wet wind in the ears, spinning through the deep dark between the hedges.

Please please God, Father, Son and Holy Ghost, let everything get all right.

SIX

And Lo! There was an Angel

Veritas was back from the hospital late, but burbling with bounce and seasonal cheer. She had an extra turkey perched on the front passenger seat of the van, another boxful of tangerines, even more crackers to add to the dozens keeping dry in the linen room, and the thirty-two pink-and-white sugar mice that were needed for putting in the stockings.

I was glad I'd managed to say nothing emotional and personal to Tommy about the distressing cot scene in hospital because I'd be having to retract it. Our father was not so very ill after all. He was beginning to get better. By the very next day, he was reported to be sitting up sipping broth. By the end of the week, Veritas told us, he'd been taken off the Danger List, and we had to believe her because her Latin name meant truth.

'And if he spends the spring somewhere really warm and sunny so his lungs can dry out, he'll be quite strong again,' she said, beaming. 'Maybe North Africa? We've always wanted to go to Tunis. That's where the tangerines come from. Father says people never get asthma in the desert.'

'What about us? Will we come?' Alfred George asked anxiously.

'An' me?' lisped Blanche.

'Me too?' squeaked Felicity like a sad pale mouse.

I said, 'What about Granny?'

'Oh she'll definitely come too,' said Veritas.

So the distant future was all settled and we could carry on with getting ready for Christmas. Even having to go to school while the rich children stayed at home having fun didn't seem quite so annoying.

At school, too, there was plenty of Christmas activity which made a reasonable distraction from trying to learn. There was wet steamed plum pudding for dinner and auditions to see who should read aloud at the Carol Service. When I told Veritas I'd been chosen, she was pleased out of all proportion to the distinction.

'I *am* glad you got given the job!' she said. 'That definitely deserves an extra bun for tea.' Her reward system was odd. I would have preferred a pocket money rise.

'Job?' I said.

'Didn't you say you were going to be reading one of the bible lessons?'

'It's not a *job*. It's just a thing that one person from each class does. Our class reads the coming of the angel Gabriel to the Virgin Mary.'

'What thrilling news!' she insisted. 'Father will be proud. Shall I tell him when I go in this evening, or would you rather tell him yourself on Sunday?' On Sundays, the hospital allowed children on to the ward. Perhaps they believed that the dangers of us introducing outside infections was less on the Lord's own day. 'You know Ruthie, I always hoped you might become an actress one day.'

I said, 'But Mum, it's not because I was the best. Muriel Pogle was. They only chose me because of Father.'

'That's right! Inherited talent. He used to do a lot of radio work during the war. And in films. He was usually a stand-in. He never actually had a speaking role.'

'Not because of that. Because they think it'll cheer me up.'

Veritas looked surprised. She stopped wrapping presents for the holiday guests and put her arms round me. 'Dearest Ruthie! I had no idea you were unhappy. You seemed so chirpy.'

'I *am* chirpy,' I said. 'Well, perhaps not *that* chirpy, none of us are. But don't you see? Usually the class votes on who's going to do it. This time they weren't allowed to. During our auditions, the headmistress came and the teachers did a lot of whispering. They couldn't decide between me and Muriel Pogle.' It had been obvious, through the glass door, that they were having trouble working out whether a sick father or a burned plait was more worthy of compensation.

Muriel Pogle had looked quite put out. Later, when she was crying in the cloakroom, I saw her comforted by her cronies who would certainly have voted for her if the auditions had not been rigged.

'Don't you want to do it? Because if you don't, you must

definitely tell your Miss Thingy that you don't feel up to it.'

'Of course I'm up to it. It's a great honour. You get to have your dinner at First Sitting, and when we go into the hall for the service, you sit in a special place, and when it's your turn to read, you walk right down the middle of the whole school, past the prefects, the head girl, the teachers and the special visitors. And everybody is totally quiet, listening to you. But I'd rather know I was doing it because I'd been elected as the most suitable.'

'You *are* suitable, Ruth. You've got a lovely reading voice and you look very nice, so long as you remember to stand up straight and not to slouch.'

'But I know, and *Muriel* knows, and the teachers all know, probably by now the whole town knows, that I'm only a runner-up. I've been chosen because they decided to feel *sorry* for me. Don't you see how awful that is?'

Veritas didn't. 'It's good for your character to have to suffer a bit,' she said. This was also her reply when I'd asked for a pocket money rise in order to cope with Christmas. 'It's not only good for your character, but people much prefer a handmade present. They can see you've put a bit of yourself into it.'

So I stumped off to finish making my cards for the aunts, uncles and godparents. This year's style was cut-out, stand-up angels, rosy-cheeked, with curls, halos and wing-tips picked out in gold. I drew their hands pressed prayerfully together in front of their flat sexless chests. I painted their eyes gazing upwards in what I thought was a rather clever attitude of holiness. My father had seen me at work on them before he was taken to the hospital. He'd said that I'd definitely captured the true spirit of Christmas since they all looked pleasantly drunk. It was his approval that made me carry on now.

I showed Mary, wanting more admiration.

'Hm. Very nice,' she said without even looking up. She was too busy designing her own card, a festive rodent reclining in a bower of white Christmas roses.

After the earlier mouse-trouble, she'd turned her affection away from mice towards rats, not any old rats, but so-called champagne-hooded ones. They had fawn-coloured markings round their necks, thick scaly tails and razor-sharp, yellow teeth. Mary sketched the large male as it sniffed round her paintbox.

'Isn't he so lovely?' she said. The ugly artist's model was savaging the festive flowers among which it was supposed to nestle. I felt that in her picture Mary was making her pet appear far more endearing than it was in life. Perhaps this would be true of any creature she decided to love.

I returned to my own genderless messengers from heaven. Alfred George came to have a look.

'Like the gold paint,' he said.

'Don't fiddle,' I said, though I felt pleased for it wasn't often he approved of something I owned or did.

'Where d'you get it?'

'Woolies. Ninepence.'

'Why have you made their eyes like that?'

'Like what?'

'Rolling round in their heads. Are they meant to be

delirious? Mary said when you saw Father, he was delirious and his eyes rolled round.'

I snatched back my cards. 'Of course they're not meant to be delirious,' I snapped. 'Angels don't get ill. They're supposed to be looking holy. Anybody with any spirituality in them could see it.'

These holidays, I was sharing my bedroom with Boodor, the daughter of a rich Persian. Or rather, my room had become Boodor's and she was kindly sharing it with me. She was fourteen, large and perpetually tired. She was scared of hairy creatures so my cats were banned from the room, which seemed especially harsh when the weather was so cold.

'It's not as though she's really allergic,' I complained to Veritas on behalf of my cats.

'Maybe not,' said Veritas. 'But she's in a foreign country and we must do all we can to make her feel at home.'

Boodor was rumoured to be a princess. But Veritas was such an ardent royalist she might have been misinterpreting a rich father for a royal one.

Personally, I thought that a friendly purring cat or two would be just the right companion to relieve the pangs of homesickness.

Boodor spent most of each day lying on my bed (which was now her bed) leafing listlessly through my collection of dog-eared women's magazines. At least the old magazines were still mine. For the duration of the holiday, I slept on a canvas camp-bed from my father's distant army days. Boodor only cheered up at meal-times. She was impressed by the variety and quantity of food being stockpiled in the larder, the pantry and the outhouses, though was perplexed by the crafty handiwork we were doing.

'Why you are not purchasing good gifts?' she asked, as she watched me making a lily-of-the-valley decorative pin-on brooch from green wool, wire and candle wax. That's what the instructions said you needed in the *Gifts for Girls* booklet.

I tried to explain Veritas's beliefs. 'She says it's more of a surprise if you give something unique that a person couldn't possibly get anywhere else.'

The lily spray for Cook was certainly turning out to be as unique as it was horrible, partly because I was having to use angora wool which made the stems soft and fluffy. I knew real lilies-of-the-valley have sleek shiny stems. They grew in May under the trees in the lower orchard.

'Then you will help me, please,' said Boodor. 'And I too will create a gift.'

I said, 'Well, one quick way is if you do half and half. Buy something and then improve it with your own personal handiwork.'

I knew she had plenty of pocket money because I'd seen the Cash/Accounts pocket book where Veritas kept a tally of which child was to supposed to get what.

What I had in mind for Boodor to buy and improve upon was something like the white handkerchief I'd bought in Woolies for thruppence and upon which I was embroidering a personal cross-stitch message in order to give it to one of the holiday nannies.

Boodor soon got the idea. On the next shopping expedition to town, she bought the ingredients for pink Turkish delight squares and golden honeycomb chunks. She made several pounds of both and consumed them in bed. The ingestion of so much sugar made her light-headed and carefree. She showed me the photo of a boy which she kept in her school trunk. He was as chubby and shiny as herself with smudgy dots for eyes peeping out of the puppy-fat cheeks.

'Is he your brother?'

Boodor giggled. 'My betrothed,' she said. 'My very beloved.'

'D'you miss him a lot?'

She shook her head and explained that the pudgy boy was her husband-to-be and she'd only met him once before her father had sent her away to an English boarding school to pass the time until she was sixteen and old enough for the marriage.

I felt dizzy with panic, for myself as much as her. Boodor was only a year older than me, yet already her future was settled. My own vague thoughts about sleek imaginary men in fast cars seemed childishly immature.

'Are you er, you know, sort of in love with him?'

'Not yet. It is not the time. But when it is the time, love will be there for me. My father is a good man. He has chosen wisely for me.'

Such trust. I would not trust either of my parents to choose anything wisely for me, let alone a beloved to last a lifetime.

While Boodor's father made money in the Middle East, mine remained in his hospital bed. At least they'd moved him out of the undignified cot.

'Just over Christmas Day. To keep him out of the way,' Veritas said. 'It'll be easier all round.' And she urged us to direct our do-it-yourself skills towards creating presents for him too.

I decided to decorate a beer bottle for him. The pint of pale ale would be disguised as Mother Christmas, with papiermâché head, painted cardboard hat, gathered red skirt, and outstretched paper arms. But, like the woolly lily-of-the-valley, it did not work out as conceived. Instead of smiling cheerfully, Mother Christmas's face leered lopsidedly and her paper arms were not stretching eagerly out but hung limply at her sides. Poor Mother Christmas was not only delirious like the angels, but semi-paralysed.

'Never mind, Ruthie,' said Veritas. 'You know it's the thought that counts and I'm sure Father will love it anyway.'

Meanwhile, parcels containing more orthodox presents were arriving by every post. The heap beneath the tree spread outwards across the hall like a relentless volcanic lava flow. Most were for the visitors, but a few were addressed to my family or to the household. There was a delivery by special courier from a *confiseur et chocolatier* in Mayfair of a casket shaped like a miniature chest-of-drawers in a presentation basket. The accompanying card was extravagant:

'*For all the darlings to enjoy! Longing to catch up with your news!! Have a simply gorgeous time at Xmas!!! Sure you will! Loads o'love, D!!!!*'

'Ah, dear Denise,' sighed Veritas. 'So generous. It's wonderful how she keeps in touch.'

I didn't think that one delivery of chocolates, however expensive they were, counted as keeping in touch. Nor did it seem particularly generous when the contents had to be shared round thirty-three people. There were three drawers in the little chest, with nine luscious chocolates in each, which meant that we could each enjoy four-fifths of a chocolate or six people could go without.

Blanche said, 'Cuthing chocolate ith difficult. You got to have a tharp knife for that.'

Cook said, 'All this chocolate! I don't hold with it. It's bad for their health.'

Christmas Day turned out to be normal, like the pictures on the cards. Stockings at 5 am, church for everybody (except the Muslims who stayed behind with two of the nannies and laid the tables), presents, turkey, sixpences in the pudding. Normality ended shortly after the Queen's speech on the wireless. Then, while our guests worked off the pain of their extended stomachs with jolly games of charades and sing-songs songs round the tree (with the exception of Boodor who lay on the sofa slowly and dreamily eating her way through all three layers of Denise's chocolates), Veritas, Mary, Alfred George, Blanche, Felicity and I prepared for our hospital visit.

'I want you to look as *beautiful* as you can,' Veritas said.

'Father won't be interested in what we're wearing,' I said. 'He never is.' The only thing he minded about was clean fingernails.

Veritas said, '*He* may not mind. But think of the other

patients. They won't want to see a scruffy gang of kids clumping in. But if you all look nice, it'll cheer them up and help them to get better more quickly.'

So Mary and I made a great effort with polished shoes, clean white stockings and ironed ribbons in our well-brushed hair.

Veritas herself was wearing new nylons, new black suede shoes, a red velvet dress with white fur trimmings on the collar and a huge gathered skirt like a merry-go-round. Apart from the wayward hair springing up in all directions like fire-crackers, I thought she looked very nice and told her so.

'A bit like Snow White, except your face is round more than heart-shaped.'

Boodor and I had been studying an article in one of my magazines about how to determine the shape of your face and get the most out of it. There were more face-shapes than we realised: square, round, pear, strong-jawed, broad-browed. Heart-shaped was definitely the one to aim for.

Veritas dressed her littlest daughters in impractical matching party frocks, specially bought for this afternoon, with fluffy petticoats, frilled yokes and satin sashes.

'Very fetching!' said Cook. 'Like a pair of tinsel fairies off the tree.'

Alfred George put on one of our father's ties with his own grey flannel school shirt.

It seemed strange and exciting to set out on a journey on Christmas afternoon when the rest of the world was indoors with their fires and trees and iced cakes. Veritas drove the van cautiously along the silent, sparkling lanes.

The frosty air in the back of the van brought out the pink in all our cheeks, even in little Felicity's normally china-pale face. We all looked radiantly wholesome as we bounded like a litter of puppies across the car park.

We were stopped abruptly by a petty rumpus outside the men's ward. The Nursing Sister popped out of the sluice-room and barred our way in.

'I'm sorry dear,' she said to Veritas. 'But you can't bring all these children in here.'

'Yesterday the nurse said Christmas Day visiting would be the same as a Sunday.'

'That's right. Two at a time allowed in and only the over-twelves.'

'They're his children. They want to see their father.'

'I'm sorry, dear, but I'm on duty and rules are rules.'

So I waited outside with the three smaller ones while Veritas and Mary went in. Further down the corridor we could hear the jollity of a noisy ward of young men with nothing worse than broken limbs to recover from. Blanche and Alfred George had a sliding race down the middle of the shiny corridor. Then Felicity and Blanche twirled and whirled in their new frilly frocks. Two young nurses came past.

'Ooh, don't they looked sweet!' cooed one.

'Aah,' said the other.

After a few minutes, the Sister from our father's ward let us all in after all. She must have felt sorry for us.

'Just a short visit, you understand,' she told me with a tight smile.

The ward was draped with some sad, droopy paper-chains and a faded paper bell. The atmosphere was of false and temporary gaiety. The people in the beds looked old and frail and very sick. We placed our rustic presents on the bedside locker. Our father didn't open them, and scarcely even moved his head to look at them.

For all the getting beautifully dressed up as an aid to recovery, our presence did little to cheer up anybody on the ward. After four minutes, our father had obviously had more than enough of his family.

Even before the Sister asked us to leave, Veritas said, 'Father's feeling a bit tired now.' So we trooped out again, smiling and waving, less like a litter of dogs, more like a troupe of seasoned variety performers who know when their act has been a failure.

As we went through the swing doors I glanced back for a last look and saw him leaning against his pillows with his eyes closed in relief, his long pale hands lying motionless on the sheet as though carved from marble. He looked gaunt. Even his moustache seemed to be wilting.

'Now *wasn't* that nice!' Veritas said brightly as we piled back into the van.

SEVEN

Death by Dying

The next day Veritas said, conspiratorially, 'Listen, Ruth, I'll be popping over to visit Father again this afternoon. So why don't you come along too?'

She hadn't asked Alfred George. So what was there about me visiting him that was so important? We knew how she liked to move furtively between us, telling each different things, pretending to each we're her favourite when we all know, well Mary knows and she told me, that Alfred George has always been her superduper fave and there's no contest in the matter.

'No, I don't think so, thanks,' I said, offhand. 'They'll only make me wait out in the corridor like last time. I'll come on Sunday with the others.'

'Very well,' she said reluctantly. 'You may be right about it.'

And what did she think I might be right about?

'Though it's a pity when you keep putting things off. I suppose it's your age.'

'What d'you mean?' I didn't like this implication that I was a procrastinator.

'If you put things off that you don't want to do, you sometimes never get the chance later on.'

'I never put things off! I'm *always* doing things, always helping Cook and Pauline in the kitchen. I must have peeled about a million potatoes after breakfast. And when I'm not doing things for Cook, I'm helping with the younger ones. Ever since elevenses I've been supervising a painting competition.'

Indeed, I wanted her to know, it was because I *didn't* put things off that I felt now was not a good moment to go visiting the sick. In these days immediately after Christmas, there were many things that had to be done, and had to be done now while the time was right.

There was planning our ambush on the local fox-hunters on their Boxing Day outing, for when they came cantering across the landscape hallooing and blowing their horns and letting all their slobbering hounds run amok in our garden upsetting my cats and Mary's dogs. Then there was the mud-fight tournament in the stream to be organised. The mud had to be the right texture for slinging, which involved diverting the stream into a pool, and there had to be enough dry blankets in the meadow to wrap people up in if they got blue with the cold. There was also the variety entertainment show in the attic for New Year's Eve to be rehearsed.

And also there was the dull chore of writing thank-you letters which still had to be seen to. I had to thank my former primary school teacher, to whom I'd sent one of my pious angel cards, for her gift of soap, the youngest nanny for some hair ribbon, Cook for a cellophane bagful of bath salts which was like chunky pink gravel and didn't dissolve properly so you had to be careful how you sat down in the water, Aunt Charité for more soap (hard and yellow), and Aunts Thrift and Speranza for the correspondence compendiums which each had sent. I wondered if both aunts, Thrift and Speranza, would be offended if they received the same wording of thanks since this would save me a bit of creative effort. I wasn't sure how often they met and whether they discussed mail received from nieces.

Aunt Thrift's pochette of a dozen pale mauve envelopes with matching sheets of paper were overpoweringly scented with a sticky smell that claimed to be Parma violets. Aunt Speranza's set was white and unscented, although it contained two sheets of paper for every one envelope, suggesting one was meant to write longer letters. I decided the thank-yous to all three aunts could be nearly identically worded except for 'very useful present' to Aunt Speranza, and 'deliciously aromatic present' to Aunts Thrift and Charité.

But first I went upstairs, lay on my bed and jotted down some quick reminder notes in the Personal Journal so there'd be no danger of being accused by Veritas of being a putter-offer.

26th December, Boxing Day
Urgent Things to be done (not to be put off):

Thank-you letters. Aunts etc.
Fox-hunt
Show
See about the Mud & Blankets

Under the list, I wrote: *Why's she always on at me? Why not the others?*

And I would have written more irritated fumings about Veritas but Boodor came lumbering wearily in. I remembered that, for the time being, this was her room more than mine, and also her bed. I stopped writing the journal, returned to my camp bed and did the letters.

When Boodor saw the Parma violets compendium, she became quite lively.

'So lovely,' she sighed, sniffing deeply at the envelopes. So I gave her the whole packet to keep and she lay back holding it to her nose while I wrote my letters of thanks on the plain paper from the other compendium. Perhaps the thick sickly smell reminded her of chocolate.

Later, while we were rehearsing the show up in the attic, I heard through the rattling roof tiles, the sound of the van's engine being cranked into life. It was Veritas setting off to the hospital. I should have gone with her. I knew it in my bones, just as Mary had known other things for months. But I'd said, No, not today, and got on with the things that seemed more important. Or more fun. Or less harrowing.

It was still dark in Boodor's/my room, like the middle of the night. Big Boodor was breathing heavily. And someone else was in the room with us. Was it the Axeman of the country lanes? Or the Grim Reaper?

No, the intruder was blowing gentle baby breezes on to my face.

'Ruthie, Ruthie, get up, get up! You got to wake up now!'

It was Felicity with tousled hair but solemn wideawake face, standing beside the camp-bed, pushing it with her body so that the frame rocked slurpily from side to side. The canvas was low-slung and she seemed to tower over me, a three-year-old whispering giantess, trying to rouse me when I wanted to be asleep.

'What d'you want?' I grumbled.

Felicity took my hand and squeezed it. 'Come on Ruthie, come on. Please wake up soon. Mumma's got a special sumfing she wants to tell you. Very important.'

What kind of important things do people have to tell each other at this time of night, even before the sour winter dawn has broken? Of course I knew already, just as I knew that Veritas had been right and there were some things which, if you put off, you never again got the chance to do.

So I stumbled up out of the canvas hammock slung between the hard wooden poles, and followed as she pattered ahead, barefoot, in her long woollen nightie, leading the way along the chilly passages to our parents' room. Sleeping children and staff were behind every door. Nobody else was up yet, not even Cook. Her door was closed. No light shining under it. She was still dreaming of the big breakfast fry-ups: scrambled eggs, fried eggs, fat sausages, thin sausages, streaky bacon, back bacon, grilled tomatoes, fried bread, mushrooms, beans. Mary and I usually lent a hand with the porridge and toast. Guests could have as many breakfasts as they wanted, and often did.

The bedside lamps were on in our parents' room. Veritas had already called the others and had them huddled round her on the bed, like small human rocks to protect her against the pounding of the storms.

Mary and Blanche moved up to make room for me. Another orphaned rock under the eiderdown. Veritas said, 'There you are then, Ruthie. So if we all stick together, it'll be all right.'

So he'd died, quite alone, in the bleak dog-hours of the night without any of us there to help him, nobody beside him to show him the way, not even a nurse to hold his hand and tell him it was going to be all right, just the leering painted face of Mother Christmas in her pint pot.

'I didn't want to wake you,' Veritas seemed to apologise to me. 'But I knew you'd want to know.'

Of course I wanted to know. We had to know. It was our right to know. We were his beloveds. We were his orphans.

'I wanted you to know before everybody else. But they'll have to be told. And we'll have to put it in *The Times*. And the *Telegraph*.'

'Oh, not the *Telegraph*!' said Mary. '*Please*.'

Since Mary had such firm opinions on how the morning news should be disseminated, she was the one delegated to carry out the dreadful jobs of waking Cook, then the two young nannies, and the three general all-purpose helpers.

And who would tell the holiday children that one of their house-parents was dead?

Veritas said, 'Perhaps Cook can tell each one separately when she asks them what they want for their breakfast. That'd be best, wouldn't it?'

It grew light. Felicity, usually so solemn, hopped brightly off the bed to open the curtains, hippity hoppity like a white fluffy little bird.

'Sunny sunshine!' she said. Perhaps she was still too young to understand what had happened overnight.

'Thas not thunthine,' contradicted Blanche, who was a whole eleven months older so reckoned she knew more about weather. 'Thas pouring.'

In fact, it looked as though it was going to be a sour yellowish sort of day.

Veritas said, 'When she grows up, she won't even remember him, will she? In a year's time she'll have forgotten her own father.'

'Oh but she *will* remember,' Mary said. 'Won't you Felicity? You can't forget your father. And if she *does* forget, then we'll tell her. Every day, we'll talk about him, what he looks like, how he speaks, what he says.'

'How he wheezes,' added Alfred George.

'And we'll show her pictures of him. If she remembers him now, she can go on remembering all her life, can't you Felicity?'

'An' me,' said Blanche.

So Mary and I saw ahead our challenging job which might

temporarily absorb grief. We had to help the baby remember.

Cook appeared in the bedroom door, flustered, with her white uniform cap on crooked and her overall misbuttoned, but smiling broadly to cover her confusion.

'Well my! And here's a sorry sight indeed,' she said. She shook her head, half laughing, half crying. The white cook's cap wobbled. 'All six of you in the bed together with those long weepy faces! You can't be coming down to breakfast looking like that, any of you. You'll scare the living daylights out of the children. I'll get May to bring you up a little something. You'll be needing your strength.'

So Cook sent up a cup of brown sugary tea for Veritas and five mugs of warm milk, later six soft boiled eggs with dainty toast fingers. Then some little bits of fruit cake, small slivers of cold turkey, dates stuffed with green marzipan. Throughout the day, these titbits on trays kept arriving, as though we were invalids who needed feeding up, rather than five healthy children and their equally robust mother. And, though at first, it felt strange even to want to eat food on the very day that a parent had stopped eating forever, hunger was just as real as death. As Boodor had already shown me, in times of sadness, eating is sometimes the only thing a person can do.

We remained marooned in Veritas's and our father's bedroom throughout the long sullen day, eating, then dozing, weeping or staring into the fire, while the everyday noises of the Christmas holidays clattered past on the other side of the door. We were like refugees from the real world. Nobody, apart from Cook, or May with a tray, or Cook's little Pauline, timid with a pot of tea, dared to come in.

It was afternoon when we finally got up. Veritas sent us off to wash our faces and dress. I braced myself to face the throng. Mercifully, the upstairs landings were empty. Everybody must be downstairs finishing lunch. I scuttled along the passages back to Boodor's/my room, fearful of having to meet anybody.

But I couldn't be alone after all for Boodor was there, lying on the bed, sucking on a bar of nougat, bright with green pistachio and red cherry pieces.

'Come,' she said, holding out a podgy paw. 'The other girls and I have made a surprise for you.'

She lead me to the bleak north-facing bathroom nearest our room. The wall above the iron bath was in the midst of an artistic transformation.

'All for you, to please you,' explained Boodor.

She showed me. They had been painting for me the most beautiful image they could imagine, a decorative freize of stick-like dancing figures in pink shoes and voluminous *corps de ballet* skirts. Boodor proudly pointed out her part in the great work. It hadn't occured to me that inside my chunky, nougat-eating Persian room-companion, might lurk a nimble, anorexic ballerina. The tears coursed down my cheeks with the sadness of Boodor's dream and the reality.

Boodor thought I was crying for my father. She lead me kindly back to our room, made me lie on her bed and tried to comfort me with a box of marrons-glacés. When that was no help, even more generously she trudged downstairs, found one of my cats and persuaded Pauline to carry it upstairs to me. But the disloyal cat had discovered how much warmer and pleasanter it was to lie by the kitchen range than on my lurching camp-bed. She slipped from my arms and kept a hostile vigil at the bedroom door. The moment it opened (it was one of the other girls coming to see if Boodor would teach them to belly-dance), the cat slipped out and back down to the kitchen.

When Boodor went off with the other girls, she offered me the treasured photo of her fiancé to keep me company.

I tried to sound grateful when I said, 'No thanks.' Though the chubby boy in black and white might have helped her through some long lonely nights in a foreign boarding school, I knew he couldn't help me.

'Because he's not mine, is he? He's yours.'

I found myself another kind of comfort. I recorded the terrible day in words.

The Personal Journal, 2nd January
Death is not a comma, it's the full stop.
How terrible it is to know that the last thing you ever did for a parent was to make him a stupid decorated beer bottle.
Putting things off: Is Veritas right?
Perhaps if I hadn't put off visiting on Boxing
Day, my presence could have saved him and he wouldn't have died?
But you never get the same chance more than once.

On that I was wrong. I _was_ about to be offered another chance. Veritas, smartly dressed in her Sunday pleated-tartan skirt, with powder round her blotchy eyes and on her shiny pink nose, tapped on the door and asked if I would go with her down to the hospital.

'I have to fill in some forms and things,' she said, very matter-of-fact. 'We could have a cup of tea in the nurses' canteen. It'd be nice if you came too.'

Nice for who? Later, I found out she'd already asked Mary but Mary wouldn't go.

'All right,' I said, for here was a second chance to put things right. 'I'd like to see him.'

'Oh no, you won't be able to do that,' said Veritas quickly. 'They'll have taken him away and put him in their chapel by now.'

'I can see him there then.'

'*I* shan't be seeing him,' she said, as though that must settle it for both of us. 'You shouldn't either.'

'Why not? You went to look at Grandfather after he died. And you told Mary and me you wished we'd seen him too. You said he looked magnificent and wonderful and it made you feel much better.'

'That wasn't the same,' said Veritas. 'Your father was very ill. He died in a different way.'

How did she mean, different? Surely dying was dying and dead was dead.

It seemed that Father hadn't slipped quietly out of life in the middle of the night. He had been found half in his bed, half falling out, as though tussling with the Grim Reaper.

'The ward sister says he was all over the place. It's wouldn't be right for you to see him.'

All-over-the-place was frightening. Even more, I needed to see him, whatever he looked like.

'He probably doesn't look very good. Better to remember him as he was the last time you saw him.'

Angrily, I said, 'You mean on Christmas Day, suffocating into that breathing mask?' Too weak even to look any of his children in the eye? Feebly waving his skeletal hand, signalling us to leave him alone? Surely nobly dead was a better last image?

Veritas said sharply, 'Sometimes it seems to me as if you don't really care about anything except yourself. It looks as though this hasn't affected you one bit.'

I could have rummaged under my pillow and shown her my journal. Then she'd know if I cared or not.

I decided against it. Some things had to remain private.

So Veritas had the last word and went off to sign papers on her own. He was her husband. She was the widow. I was only a daughter. That was a good deal lower down the scale.

Personal Journal, 3rd January

Glad I said nothing. We're on to wreath-making now.

EIGHT

Our Fathers Which Art in Heaven

<u>Personal Journal</u>

Still January 3rd and it's still true.

*He died too early in the morning. He shouldn't have died so early.
There's been the whole of that first morning to get through. Then the
middle part of that day.*

*Then that terrible long afternoon watching the girls painting their
pink dancing stick-insects on the bathroom wall.*

*And the evening. That was terrible. And the going to bed at the end
of the first day. That was even worse, specially when Boodor said she'd
get one of my cats brought up. It was nice of her to offer but I know
she doesn't like them in the room.*

*Neither do the cats. Perhaps it's the smell of Parma violets puts
them off.*

Waking on the morning of the second day, it had to be
remembered all over again: he's dead. Then there was the
whole of that day to be got through. Then the whole of the
fourth of January which was day three.

In the Bible, on the third day, He rose again. Our father didn't (even though I prayed and prayed that it would all be a bad dream and I'd soon wake to normality).

I woke to the fourth day. Which had to be endured. And the fifth. And every other day until the funeral.

Muslims cremated their dead, Boodor told me, more quickly, within twenty-four hours. If that was Allah's way, I preferred it. None of this hanging around. But Veritas said we needed this time to get ready. What getting-ready could there possibly be?

'Making wreaths,' she said.

She wanted us to weave, or bind or somehow create our own personal wreaths.

'You'd like to, wouldn't you?' she said encouragingly. 'Yes of course you would. It'll be so much nicer. And people will know you really care.'

I said, 'But how can we make them ourselves? We're not trained florists. We don't know how.' There was a very old woman in the village who'd worked in Covent Garden long ago. She gave a talk to the Mother's Union. I'd been to it with my grandmother. Ethel said she'd been training for over six months before they'd even let her so much as bunch up the violets with the raffia.

Veritas laughed off my doubts. 'Don't worry so much. It'll be easy, and such fun. I'll get them to send some stuff from the flower shop.'

So circular wire frames, a sack of dry moss, a roll of green florists' twine, and some small perky bunches of paperwhites, sunny yellow jonquils, and bright anemones, were delivered. Mary and I set to work in the larder where it was cool so the blooms wouldn't wilt.

Making wreaths turned out to be just as difficult as I'd thought it would be. The flower-heads snapped off however gently you tried to wire them into graceful position. The greenery from the florist was too springy to be manageable. The dried moss crumbled like broken biscuits and there wasn't nearly enough of it to hide the wire. I went out into the garden and scraped more moss off a tree trunk. But it was the wrong type and seething with distressed woodlice. Soon the few surviving flower petals were muddy and the wreath was a crumpled mess of dirty greenery, clinging to a mass of untidy wire knots which looked more like a floral insult than any kind of loving tribute.

'Why's she making us do this?' I grumbled at my stupid wreath. 'It's worse than the homemade presents.'

'It's something to do with the war,' Mary said calmly.

How could it be? Veritas's war-work hadn't been anywhere near a poppy-making factory. She'd driven army trucks and ambulances.

'No, not to do with what *she* did,' Mary said. 'To do with what we didn't have. You remember.'

'No.' How could I? I'd been three when the war ended.

'Yes, but it went on for years after. You know, when there was no butter or cake or furniture or clothes or curtains. So they had to make things out of nothing. It's the nostalgia makes her want to go on doing it.'

And also, as I knew full well, she believed that a bit of suffering was good for our character development. I said, 'People are going to laugh if they see this.'

'But if it's making her feel better,' Mary said soothingly, 'then we must go along with it.'

Alfred George entered into wreath-making with a greater gusto. He stomped off down the lane, carried back two chunks of wood, bound them together with string from his personal rope and string collection to form a rugged rustic cross which he draped with swags of ivy. I was envious. He had achieved natural simplicity with seemingly little effort and no green wire. Was it because he was a boy? Were boys actually better than us? Or were things just easier for them?

He wrote a message on a piece of paper and tied it to the ivy.

'Hello Father, hope you're having a nice tim as a star (That's What Felicity Says You Are anyhow) Love from us All specialy and HIgly Respectfully, Your Son Alfred George.'

With unusual generosity, he invited the two younger sisters to attach their own messages to his cross. Bubbling Blanche got one of the nannies to write for her.

'Father, Stay with us always. love, Blanche, X X X.'

'That's really cruel!' I said. 'Letting her put that. It'll make her think he's not really gone, that he's still here, and that he's coming back soon.'

Mary, calm as ever, pointed out that since Blanche couldn't read, she probably had no idea what the nanny had written on her behalf.

Baby Felicity did her own message with coloured crayons on a long sheet of foolscap typing paper. Since Felicity couldn't write any more than Blanche could read, nobody knew what it actually said. But it was as swirly and scribbly as a bright rainbow whirlwind.

While we were struggling in the cold larder with our wire and bits of wood, the holiday staff, Cook, the nannies, the domestics, the man who dug the garden, and Tommy, the boy who helped him, had a whip-round for their late employer. Johnnie, one of the boys who'd been coming to stay every holiday since he was ten, organised a collection among the other child guests. Then he and another of the older boys delegated themselves to telephone from our father's study for a taxi to take them into town to commission their wreath. When it was delivered, it stood as tall as a seven-year-old and was breathtakingly extravagant. Each child had specified their favourite colour. The wreath-maker had obligingly woven a paintbox riot, even brighter than Blanche's whirlwind, of daffodils, chrysanthemums, anemones, zinnias, roses, irises of two types, freesias, carnations, bell hyacinths, and more. Every contributor's name was inscribed on a black-edged card invisibly wired on.

How I envied them the professionalism of their wreath. How I longed to be one of them, to add my name to their card and cast my own miserable mess of wire and dying blooms on to the compost heap.

Funeral fixed for tomorrow. About time too. Iron hair ribbons.
Wash hair. Polish shoes. Find clean stockings.
Q. Is there anything worse than a badly decorated Christmas beer
bottle?
A. Yes, a homemade wreath that hasn't worked out. It is shaming. I
am just glad that he can't see it. Or can he?

'Know what, Ruth?' Johnnie said to me as he slicked down his hair with Brilliantine. 'I thought I'd have to wait years for a chance like this. But this'll be the first funeral I've ever been to! It's beastly grim about your pa and all that, but it'll be brilliant telling them about it next term.'

For Johnnie, this death culminating in burial, was the best entertainment that Veritas had so far organised, outclassing the trip to the pantomime, the New Year's Eve dance and even the mud tournament.

All the children came to the church, including Boodor and the two Kuwaiti brothers whose God was known as Allah.

'It's all right,' one of the brothers reassured me. 'He is the same God underneath.'

It was nothing like Grandfather's uplifting triumph which had vanquished all fear of death. It was bad and bleak and cold and there weren't enough people. The village church was small. It should have been full to bursting. There should have been everybody from the whole village here, from the whole nation, from the whole world to help us. A straggle of unfamiliar people in overcoats hovered round the gate under the yew trees.

'Part of father's past,' Mary whispered.

Some greeted Veritas with handshakes or formal kisses on the cheek. Some didn't seem to know her at all. The vicar was also a stranger. The real one was ill with pneumonia.

Aunts Thrift, Charité and Speranza weren't here, even though this was their own sister who was the widow, their brother-in-law who was the corpse. Perhaps they thought death was men's business. At least Uncles Falcon, Merlin and Kestrel had come, though Uncle Guillemot, the vicar, was off burying someone else in another part of the county. At least, he'd sent his eldest son as a representative. I noticed how Cousin Tern winked keenly at Mary as he got out of a car. But I wasn't sure if he'd managed to attract her attention. Unlike us, he was considered to be already grown-up. He was going into the Navy. Our grandmother had told us so.

As we trooped up the path between the ancient gravestones, I spotted Timmy with his shorthand pad and his soft pink ears, lurking in the shadows of the west porch. He was taking down names of people as they went in. I hadn't seen him about for ages.

I felt a hopeful lurch in the stomach. Obviously, he wouldn't need to ask me my name and what relationship I was to the deceased because he already knew but I wanted him to notice me, to smile at me, to say 'Hello Ruth,' as though he saw and admired the noble bravery of the way I bore sadness. I wanted him to let me know that even on a day as sad as this, I existed as a female person.

Yet, as I passed into the church, Timmy managed to make his pale sandy eyes look right through me as though I was invisible, as though I, too, were already a mere ghost of a person. Not a flicker of friendship. Had he really forgotten who I was? Or was he repaying me for my callousness when I said I wouldn't even walk down the lane with him?

The coffin was way up the front. I thought of my father lying inside that wooden box. I supposed it really was him and not some stranger's body. What was he wearing? Was it his pinstripe trousers with the long black coat which Veritas insisted he *always* wore to funerals? Or had they dressed him in his baggy corduroys, held up with his faded silk tie? The lid looked very firmly closed so now I would never know.

Veritas shepherded all twenty-three of us towards the three pews right at the back of the church. Our view was blocked by the bulk of the men in front.

'Why don't we sit up there?' I whispered. The front pews were where important family people should be. We were the chief mourners, not Falcon, Merlin and those male relations I'd never seen before.

'No, this is the best place,' Veritas insisted. 'We'll be able to see much better from here.'

Since we were sitting beside the font she'd have been quite right if it'd been our father's baptism we were coming to.

From here at the back, it hardly felt like a funeral at all, more like an ordinary service. None of us was wearing black.

None of us cried. We took our cue from Veritas and launched lustily into hymn number three-hundred- and ninety-eight.

Johnnie, with his shiny greasy quiff of hair, began belting it out as though he really meant it. '*Day of Wrath! O Day of Mourning*'. He was singing it for me. I knew it and felt grateful. It softened the snub from Timmy who'd collected his list of names and wasn't hanging about for the service. At least our father would get his paragraph in *The Weekly Express and County Tribune*.

From our places at the back, we could hear but not see the priest. He'd got to the bit where he was saying, 'For a thousand years in thy sight are but as yesterday,' when there was a rattley clatter at the main door, then a jangling like sleigh bells. I recognised the irritating noise of those gold bracelets even before I saw their owner. Like a giant raven, wearing a huge black feathered hat, in swept Denise, straight up the aisle, round Father in his box on its wooden trestles, to a place nearly at the front, as though she was the star of the programme.

What right did she have to interfere in our family's funeral when she wasn't even a relation?

'Anyone would think it was her funeral!' I muttered to Mary. 'It's so rude, showing off like that!'

'Don't take it personally,' Mary muttered back. 'She can't help it. It's her theatrical background – it makes her want to grab the limelight. At least she'll go away once it's over.'

Mary was right. I resolved to write a reminder in the P.J. *Do not Take Things (or People) so Personally*. This personal reminder might be useful for covering my confused feelings about Timmy too.

Afterwards, there was a brief mourners' tea in father's study. The teapots were on his desk, the trays of cups on his bookshelves. But there were no pretty little fancy cakes with crystallised petals on top like we ate at Grandfather's wake. Cook had obviously considered that towering mounds of doleful sardine-paste sandwiches were more appropriate. Johnnie politely handed them round to the uncles as if he was one of the family.

'Such a terrible shock for them all,' said one of the unknown non-relation men, sipping his tea and peering at our father's shelves of military archives in an acquisitive way.

'Veritas, my darling! What a simply divinely lovely service. So cheerful!' Denise gurgled through the shiny black feathers that flapped down from the brim of her hat. 'And all your adorable little orphans too. If only *everybody* could do funerals as well as you.'

As the people left in their dribs and drabs, some of them kissed Veritas goodbye. Some kissed Mary. Some kissed me. A porky, fat-faced man with thin yellow hair came up to me, shook my hand and then pressed two half-crowns into it.

'There you go, m'dear. Just a few bob to keep out the miseries, what?' he said into my ear. 'Grand chap your father, by the by. Sound fellow.'

Five shillings might be a lot of money, but could never be enough to recompense having a dead parent. I found out later that he'd given Mary the same, Alfred George ten shillings, and the little ones each a shilling.

'But who on earth was he?' I asked.

'Her cousin Roland,' said Mary.

I'd never heard of any cousin called Roland before.

'He's not really her cousin. He just calls himself that. He's known her since they were young. He used to sing in Grandfather's choir.'

I asked Veritas, 'Why did you invite that man if you haven't seen him for twenty years?'

She said, 'I didn't. It's not the done thing to invite people to a funeral. They just come if they want to.'

'Why were you so nice to him?'

'He's a solicitor. You never know, he might come in handy one day.'

'Well, I didn't like his hot breath.'

Soon after the announcement had appeared in the deaths column of *The Times*, the letters started to come. The postman had only just got over the exhaustion of delivering all those joyful seasonal greetings. Now, from the same acquaintances, came their messages of condolence. Every morning, the postman wearily thumped the big bundles, tied with hairy twine, on to the hall table.

In a lifetime, even such a curtailed one, our father must have bumped into an awful lot of people, judging by the numbers who wrote. But there was little variation in how sorrow was worded. It got quite repetitious.

We were so sorry to read of your sad loss.

We were all saddened and shocked at the sad news and feel so very sorry for you all.

I am so terribly sorry, what more can I say?

We were so terribly sorry to hear of your dear husband's death. But at least, dear Veritas, you have the comforts of a lot of children and a good philosophy on life.

'And they'll all need answering!' Veritas said unhappily. After reading the first bundle, she couldn't bring herself to open any more so they soon got muddled up with the bills from the butcher, the fishmonger and the eggman, and the stiffly worded letter from her bank manager saying there was no money left in her account after the Christmas spending spree.

'Silly fellow,' said Veritas with a laugh. 'Doesn't he understand *anything* about running a children's holiday hotel?' Few parents paid in advance, and even when they did, cheques sent from Tehran or Buenos Aires or Borneo took weeks to travel round the world and reach Sussex.

The undertakers' bill also arrived. It made more interesting reading than the letters of condolence. But it seemed that funerals come expensive, even modest ones.

' *To supplying selected waxed polished Agba Blenheim Coffin with moulded lid and plinth. Lined throughout in swansdown mattress and pillow. Fitted with interior side sheets, frill. Mounted 4 prs brass handles, backplates, closing bolts, breastplate with inscription.*

To hearse and bearers with Coffin at hospital, placing remains therein and removing to Chapel of Rest.

To supplying hearse and conveying Coffin from our Chapel of Rest to church for interment.

To Undertaker attending, making necessary arrangements.'

The total for all this was going to be thirty-four pounds and ten shillings.

I said, 'It seems to me she could've saved a bit by cutting out all that swansdown stuffing for the mattress and the pillows and frills.'

And as for the brass breastplate with inscription, we'd never even got near enough to see if it existed, let alone what it said. And now that it was buried, nobody else would either, at any rate not for thousands of years until there's an earthquake or another Ice Age.

Veritas didn't have enough money to pay the undertaker's bill. Mary found it lying on her desk three weeks later, still unpaid. Another bill had joined it. She'd gone and ordered a best quality Forest of Dean stone memorial headstone with a lot of expensive engraving and enamelling of the incised letters.

'Another twenty-one pounds and seventeen shillings.'

Mary said, 'I suppose we'll have to ask Cousin Roland. He said he'd do anything for her.'

'Oh please don't let's do that,' I begged.

NINE

New Lives for Old

For the rest of the holidays, Cook stomped around with a grim I-told-you-so look on her face. Occasionally, while carving the huge succulent sides of beef, she clicked her teeth and sighed. 'And we just don't know where all this is going to end, in truth we do not.'

But end it did. As soon as the holidays were over, and the guest-children had been sent off in taxis and trains with their well-packed trunks and tuck-boxes, our life took on another way of being. For starters, the radiators went cold and it wasn't an oversight. Veritas let the boiler burn itself out and told the man who stopped by to stoke it on his way to work at Hare's farm, not to bother.

'It'll save fuel,' she explained to me.

With no kitchen range, there could be no more juicy roasts. At mealtimes, we ate toast and jam, toast and margarine, scrambled eggs on toast, toast and very old dripping, while Veritas pounded away on the QWERTY UIOP keys of her Imperial. She had finished and was now rewriting her latest juvenile pageant, though she never knew beforehand if it was going to be performed or how much she might be paid, if ever.

With Boodor gone, I got my own bed back. One of my less disloyal cats also returned to share it, though only because she was pregnant. She went into labour on the faded flowery counterpane just as she had done several times before. The dairy farmer's wife up the hill said this was very unusual.

'You must have a real rapport with your cats, Ruth,' she said with admiration. 'Usually they find themselves a nice dark little corner out of the way for their birthings.'

This cat was already a grandmother. So as well as knowing about dark corners, she ought to have known that a mating so early in the season wasn't a good idea.

At her previous confinements, I'd been amazed to witness the biological miracle, moved by the plaintive mewings out of the snub toothless mouths, and impressed by the tender care of the mother. On one splendid occasion when she'd been producing a litter of seven, she'd attended to each new arrival with such enthusiastic care, licking and nurturing, pausing only for as long as it took to push out the next. This time, the whole business with all its mess and mucus, disgusted me. So did the cat for, halfway through, she seemed to want to give up. It was as though she'd lost interest in motherhood. The sum total of her half-hearted efforts was a litter of one, scarcely even a litter. Just a sad little singleton. She sniffed at it distastefully then wandered off to the furthest edge of my bed and turned her back on me. For the next few days, I had to remind her to feed her baby.

So, though there might be new life in this coming year, it didn't bring any rays of new hope.

Mary and I went back to school for the new term three days late. Veritas had never put a high priority on regular attendance. She'd always seized upon excuses to keep us off school. Now she seemed actively to want us near her, round her, within sight, even if she appeared to ignore us.

Now she said, 'Well, if you're really intent on going back, you better say you're late because of the funeral.'

I said, 'But that was weeks ago! And anyway it only lasted an hour.'

'Very well then. You better say it's because you've had colds and been under the weather.'

In reality, as we knew, it was because her feeling of not wanting us to go anywhere was contagious. I'd felt so lethargic that I'd failed to set my alarm clock, then, having failed to wake up in time, it seemed too difficult to get the day started. Another reason was that I couldn't find any of my school uniform. During the upheavals of making space for the holiday guests, Mary's and my navy gymslips, ties and felt hats with the crested badges on the front had been bundled into a grocery box and shoved out of the way up in the attic.

'And when you get there,' Veritas warned us, 'Don't say anything. People don't like it if you talk about sad things. You must try not to upset the other girls.'

Upset the others! I thought. And what about *my* upsets?

When I walked into the classroom of Lower IV S, twenty-nine pairs of eyes looked at me. But nobody whispered to me, Where have you *been*? Nobody asked why I didn't bring an excuse-note to lay on the form mistress's desk. She herself said nothing to me, no welcome back, no mentions of anything out of the ordinary that might have happened in the Christmas holidays, no word of sympathy, either then or ever. Nor from the headmistress, nor the deputy, nor any of the other staff.

Since we were cold-shouldered by our contemporaries, at breaktime Mary and I had to keep each other company. We met up in the playground and cowered side by side in the bike shelter. In her gaberdine pocket, Mary found a set of coloured wooden knuckle-stones she'd been given for Christmas. So we played matches against each other on the dusty ground.

Then, one breaktime while I was waiting for Mary to turn up, my vile enemy, Muriel Pogle, sidled into the bike shelter too. She'd still not forgiven me for reading at the carol concert.

'Miss Russell's told me about you-know-what,' Muriel said with an embarrassed smirk. 'And she's told me I've got to be nice to you. Actually, I already knew about it. My father saw it in the Friday *Gazette*. It means your mother's a widow now, doesn't it?'

'Yes.'

'If you think that means you're something special, you've got another think coming because it doesn't.'

I gulped. 'I don't. I mean, I didn't.'

'And another thing it said in the paper as how your mother's a very famous writer.'

'Not very famous. Just a little tiny bit, sometimes.'

'Well don't go giving yourself any fancy ideas on that score either because I'm not impressed.'

When she saw Mary approaching, she hurried out of the shelter.

Muriel was the only person in the school who allowed herself this close to mentioning that thing, the only thing, that unmentionable thing that had happened in the holidays. But even she didn't know how to follow it. And she definitely didn't know what Miss Russell meant by 'being nice' to me.

I wished it could be like the olden days when my grandmother was young, when there were careful rules of etiquette for times like this, when girls wore black dresses and ribbons for a set number of months according to how closely related they were to the departed. Then everybody would know how to behave towards us. It seemed that everybody *did* know about our father and yet it was invisible knowledge. In the P.J. I tried to make sense of it.

Personal Journal

Death is not a comma
Death is not a full stop either.
It's the long grey nothingness.
It must be like that for the dead people too.
By death, we have been ostracised.
Who is to blame?

Can I blame Muriel?

No. It's not her fault and anyway, it wouldn't help.

Shall I blame School?

Or Veritas?

Or God? (He made it happen.)

For the time being I decided not to blame anyone but instead, took my frustration out on Mary in small niggling ways.

'Hey, that's my hat you've got in your basket!' We carried our blue felt hats in our bike baskets and did not put them on until we were coming down the last hill towards the school gates where a member of staff was always standing on uniform duty, watching out for uniform evaders. 'If you can't be bothered to look for your own, don't just pick up mine.'

'I didn't.'

'Yes you did.'

'Give it here. Let me see.' When I looked inside, I saw that it was not my nametape sewn to the brim, but hers. Grumpily, I handed it back. 'Well it looks just like mine. So where's mine then?'

'How should I know?'

Though we argued on the way to school, once there we continued to stick as close as limpets. Eventually, Veritas received a warning about it from the headmistress.

'It's a reprimand,' Veritas said, showing us the letter. 'About your behaviour.'

Dear Mrs Baird,

It has come to my notice that your daughters consistently spend their free time with one another. My staff have tried to discourage them by altering their timetables. We believe it is unnatural and inappropriate for older girls to keep close company with younger girls as it can lead to detrimental situations.

While I appreciate your daughters' slightly unusual situation, this conduct cannot be an excuse for them to set a bad example to others. Please would you be so good as to remind them that in future it will be wiser for them to mix normally with the pupils from their own years rather than with one another.

Yours truly, Eunice Ramsbottom, M.A. (Oxon.)

Somehow, we dragged ourselves through the days of January. But then, there was every day of Feburary to be lived through. It may have been the shortest month but it stretched itself out like tired grey elastic. The recollection that he'd died, that he did not exist, seeped into every second of every day.

I told Mary how much I missed him.

She gave me one of her slow, wise stares to accentuate my youthful ignorance of the true facts.

'He *wanted* to be dead,' she muttered.

'Of course he didn't,' I said angrily. Why should anyone choose to be not alive?

But that evening, alone with my reluctant grandmother cat and the Personal Journal, I could find loads of reasons.

Personal Journal

One. He'd felt ill for far too long. He couldn't stand it any more.

Two. He was generally fed up with life.

Three. He lost the fight to live, the zest for living.

Four. He experienced such terrible brutal things in the First World War when he was a boy soldier that he'd been haunted by the memory for the next thirty years.

Five. His brothers and all his best friends were killed in WW1. He made some new friends, but they got killed in the Second World War so he was lonely.

Six. He wasn't in love with Veritas any more. Divorce is not possible for an officer and a gentleman (Veritas says so) so exit by death is the only way he could decently leave.

Seven. He doesn't like any of us any more. Or perhaps he never did? In which case he's the one to blame for our misery.

Mary had claimed that she'd known for two years that he was going to die. Blanche was taking it further. She insisted it was actually her fault. She was three and three-quarters years old. How could it be?

'I done it,' she said sadly but importantly, her usual bubbly bounce all subdued. 'I'th made him die. When I wath thcreaming and thcreaming in the corridor out-thide Thather's door.'

'That wasn't why he died,' I said. 'Just because you had a stupid tantrum on the floor.'

'Yeth it wath,' Blanche insisted. 'Becauth Cook come and thee told me off and thaid my thather wath tho ill and that if

I made that 'orrible noithe it wouldn't help him.'

At least Blanche's dramatic sense of personal responsibility took some of the edge off my own guilt for putting off the Boxing Day visit.

The knowledge that, in some indefinable way, it was our collective fault, was reinforced by the way Veritas's friends and relations were keeping away too. Shame hung about us like a bad smell.

The roly-poly man who called himself a cousin remained among the faithful few. So did our granny. 'I've decided I shall have to move to live nearer,' she said. 'So I can keep an eye on you. Because it's obvious your mother isn't.'

One streaming wet February night, the roly-poly cousin turned up at the front door. He wasn't expected. Mary and I both reached the hall to unbolt the door to his loud hammering at the same time.

'If he'd really have been a friend of the family he'd have known about coming round to the back,' I said. It was always left open to let the dogs in and out. We never used the front door in wintertime (except for television filming sessions but even they'd dried up) because it let in the draughts.

Cousin Roland stood on the front steps drenched with rain.

'Greetings, oh lovely ladies of youth. And how's the weather treating you? What?' he said.

I simpered. Mary scowled.

He held out a bottle of Scotch which obviously wasn't meant for either of us.

'She's not talking to anybody,' said Mary. Veritas had been shut into the study all evening, crouched over the coal fire, with our father's plaid shawl over her shoulders. She seemed to be losing interest in us, just like my poor old cat with her lonesome kitten.

'She'll talk to me, m'dear,' said Roland, handing in his whisky bottle like a visiting card.

Roland was right. Veritas would see him and she asked us to take in two glasses.

So Mary cooked the scrambled eggs on toast for our high tea and I saw the little ones to bed. Since the water was cold, I didn't bother with baths, though I filled them each a stone water bottle with warm water from the kettle. When it was time for Mary and me to go to bed, Roland was still in the study with our mother. The three of them, Roland, Veritas and the whisky stayed round the fire till long past ten o'clock.

'What's she found to talk to him about?' I wondered. 'She said yesterday she'd got nothing in common with anybody any more.'

I felt sure they must be plotting something in there. Mary thought it was more likely to do with him paying the undertaker's bill.

'In that case, surely she'd be the one giving him the whisky to say thank you?'

In the morning, Roland was still under our roof. I saw him crumpled up on the lower bunk-bed in the boys' dormitory. He looked very uncomfortable. I pedalled off to school in a huff. It was outrageous, him coming to visit and then sneakily staying when Father wasn't here. I felt like Prince Hamlet when his widowed mother married his uncle when his father had only been dead a week or so. At least Roland had gone by the time I got back from school which is more than could have been said about King Claudius.

Denise was next to pay an unannounced courtesy call. I heard the clattering bracelets and the shrill voice outside long before I saw her. She arrived in a taxi, wearing very peculiar clothes for a trip to the country, a frock-coat in shocking pink with a huge swirling skirt, and a neat little hat on one side of her head made from dozens of pink bows sewn together to look like a neat rose bush.

'Schiaparelli, darlings! Isn't it simply gorgeous? I've just been to New York. Your dear mama should go. It would do her the world of good.'

Denise brought gin, scented freesias, and a huge *Simplicity* dress pattern book.

'I would have brought the *Vogue* one but they simply wouldn't let me take it away!'

Veritas asked for two glasses and a jug of water for the flowers.

'But darlings! It's simply freezing in here!' said Denise, settling her pink skirts gracefully into one of the worn old armchairs. 'Run out and fetch some more coal, Ruth dearest, will you, or we'll all perish.'

So I picked up the scuttle and I ran and I fetched. Inappropriate though her clothes were, annoying though her mannerisms were, she brought a breath of fresh New York air with her. At least the rest of us were allowed to sit and listen in while they drank the gin. Denise had a plan, or rather several plans, for the reorganisation of Veritas's life.

'First and foremost, V dear, it's high time you changed your wardrobe. We must do something about your clothes! From top to bottom!'

'But she likes wearing Father's old rug,' I said. 'It makes her feel safe.'

Denise ignored me and flicked through the glossy pages of the dress pattern book.

'I'm sure you're good with a needle and thread, darling,' Denise said. 'So you can easily run yourself up a few little somethings. And your girls can help you with the hemming. This country life is all very well, but it's no excuse not to be smartened up or no one, but no one, will ever notice you're here.'

It seemed to me that Alfred George was in more urgent need of having his image changed. He was, as usual, wearing a very odd assembly of clothes. As well as his usual lengths of rope and the bits of useful string wound round his body, he had on a pair of our father's size twelve brogues which made it difficult for him to move, and a black velvet bolero out of the fancy-dress trunk.

'There's nothing wrong with it,' he said when I'd suggested it wasn't very suitable for a boy. 'It helps keep the chill out.'

By the time they were on to their third gins, it was clear that Denise's schemes weren't only about Veritas making new frocks. All our lives were shortly to be re-scheduled.

TEN

Shocking in Pink

As the fire crackled brightly and the level in the green gin bottle went down, so did Denise's plans unfold.

The first priority, smartening Veritas up, wasn't just to make her feel happier. It was to improve the image of the whole family, to make it more appealing. That would have to include a lot of work on Mary and me.

'They need to appear less ungainly,' said Denise. 'I mean darling, just look at them.'

I thought that Veritas hardly needed to look. She saw us every day and the only faults she regularly complained about were if we slouched, or mumbled, or held our knives and forks in the wrong hands. I had lately taken to doing all three at once. I'd got it from watching Marlon Brando, slouching over his spaghetti, slurping it up, one-handed with a fork, while mumbling out of the side of his mouth.

'No, Ruthie,' Veritas said. 'That's all very well for Chicago gangsters but it won't do for Sussex. It's fork in the left hand, knife in the right.'

'I'm sure they're charming girls, both of them,' Denise went on. 'Good complexions? Yes. Nice bone structure? Yes. Pretty hair? Well, unfashionably long unless they want to look like French Riviera starlets. I believe the gamine look is coming in. You have to admit it, they are definitely on the rustic side.'

I said, 'Hey, but what about that ambience stuff you used to say we had?'

'Poppet, that was yonks ago. So you see, Veritas, they're never going to stand a chance unless you start work on them now.'

'Stand a chance of what?' I said.

'Of finding decent husbands, duckie.'

'Husbands?' I squawked into my mug of milk and practically choked.

'Yes, darling girl.' Denise spoke loudly and slowly as though explaining to a deaf foreigner or a very uncouth country girl. 'You know, men, M.E.N. You do want to get married, don't you?'

'I suppose, one day. Maybe. Not now. I'm only in the Lower IV.' If it wasn't legal for me to leave school yet, I was pretty sure it couldn't be legal for me to marry. Even in Boodor's country where girls could marry at fourteen, her father was letting her hang on in girlhood for another two years.

Blanche said, 'I fthink my thister wanths to be a nun.'

'Be quiet, Blanchie. I didn't say that. I merely said that if I went to live in a convent, at least I'd get a cell of my own and I wouldn't have to share.'

Blanche said, 'If you geth married you hath to share your bedwoom.'

I said, 'So that's another jolly good reason against it. Luckily, I don't know anyone so there's no danger of it happening.'

'That's just the point, sweetie. You don't know anyone and no one knows you. So the sooner we can get you and Mary launched into the world, the better for everybody. You must definitely start being shown to your best advantages.'

She was talking about us as though we were prize animals. I said, in a calm reasonable voice, 'So why couldn't you wait till we're the proper age for marriage before we're shown off?'

Denise rolled her eyes in an exaggerated way to show how frustrating it was being interrupted by an ignorant uncouth wretch. 'A girl has to be ready, waiting at the starting post. Ahead of the herd.' She obviously saw us as racing cows.

'Why?'

Veritas said, 'Do at least listen to what Denise has to suggest, Ruth.'

Mary nudged me to shut up too. 'Don't keep asking her questions,' she hissed. 'You're only egging her on. It's just the gin talking anyway.'

But it wasn't. Denise was in earnest when she explained, 'The sooner you're both off your mother's hands, the better chance *she* stands. You see sweetheart, out there in the real world, no man with any sense is going to be looking twice at a widow with four daughters. But with only two very small ones she might stand a chance of throwing the double.'

Now it was beginning to sound more like Monopoly than cow racing.

Mary and I popped out to get some bread to make toast for the little ones' supper. As we put bread, margarine, knife and toasting fork on a tray, I said, 'Why does she listen to all that woman's silly drivel?'

Mary said, 'Don't take it so seriously. She's lonely. She needs someone grown-up to gossip with now and then. It's not real talk.' I thought how Mary was so much wiser and calmer than I'd ever manage to be.

Veritas and Denise were on to their fourth gins and Blanche and Felicity, full of toast, were nodding off in front of the fire, tangled up among the snuffling dogs, before Denise got round to the next important issue on her agenda. The essential plan for Alfred George was more clear-cut, though just as bizarre. He must be sent far away to a boarding school.

'As soon as possible. It's not right for him to stay here any longer. Surrounded by women! You, his grandmother living practically next door, *and* four sisters! And from what I've heard even his headteacher is female.'

Veritas said, 'But he's very happy down in the village. Miss Bodger's a lovely lady. That's where Blanche and Felicity will go when they're old enough. Everybody *adores* Miss Bodger.'

This wasn't entirely true. Some of the children were terrified of her, specially her use of the leather strap as a learning aid for teaching not very bright people to read. It hadn't worked very well with my brother either.

'The village school! All those country bumpkins from four to fourteen jammed into one stuffy class?'

I said, rather sarcastically, 'Actually, that was in the 1920s.

They've invented secondary schools now. You only stay with Miss Bodger till you're eleven.'

'Local schooling's all very well when they're little, but not for ever.'

I said, 'If it's all right for Mary and me, why won't it do for him?'

'Sweetie-pie, it's quite different for boys, especially when they're the head of the family. He needs a proper masculine education, a nice exclusive little place where he'll have the influence of strong men.'

Veritas nodded enthusiastically. I wondered how she could even pretend to think of banishing her favourite from the bosom of the family.

'I've already spoken to your cousin Roland and it's what he thinks too,' Denise said, as though that settled the matter. 'He has your best interests at heart, you know,' she added.

Veritas was worrying how this exclusive schooling was going to be paid for. 'It's very good of you to try to help, Denise. But who's going to foot the bill for all these changes?'

'You get some sort of pension, don't you?'

Denise obviously hadn't a clue about real life. I said, 'The widowed mother's pension ought to be called the widow's mite because that's all it is.' It was seven pounds and ten shillings a week.

'Don't worry,' Denise said airily. 'We'll think of something. It needn't be a very *exclusive* school. Not one where royalty goes. Perhaps he could get a scholarship?'

'I doubt it. Alfred George doesn't read yet so he wouldn't

do too well in any formal type of exam if there were question papers to be read.'

Denise wasn't surprised. But then she knew so little about children, she obviously didn't know that by nearly nine, most people usually could read.

'But he can write very well,' Veritas said proudly. 'And sing. And paint, and make bows and arrows. And tie wonderful knots in rope. He knows dozens of knots. He's invented some of his own too. And he plays the violin quite beautifully.'

I thought it might have been good if he could've known how to bring in the coal beautifully, or wash up with finesse but, like learning to read, those weren't among the useful crafts of life he'd yet mastered.

'Plays the violin?' Denise perked up. 'Marvellous! That's the answer. He can go to that special hot-house college for budding violinists.'

Alfred George said, 'But I don't much like the violin. I like climbing trees and digging tunnels better.'

I said, 'You're head of the family now. So you may have to do a *few* things you don't like.'

Veritas said, 'Even if he won a scholarship, it wouldn't cover all the costs. Most of these places have lots of hidden extras you have to pay for.' We knew about hidden extras because of the many strange things the holiday guests had to have to put in their trunks.

'Don't worry, darling. We'll think of something. If necessary, you can write begging letters to your relations. And for the time being, I'm sure you must have something we can sell?'

Denise cast her mascaraed and eye-linered eyes round the study. Thanks to all that coal I'd valiantly lugged in under her instruction and heaped on to the grate, the room was really cosy now. But apart from the radiant glow from the fire, there was little she could fasten on that was of any lasting monetary value – two broken-down armchairs on which she and Veritas sat, a threadbare carpet cast off from Grandfather's rectory on which Blanche and Felicity lay sleeping, three cats, two dogs, a free-range lop-eared rabbit (Blanche's) hiding under the desk, a portrait of one of our father's ancestors half-falling out of its frame, an aboriginal boomerang hanging from a nail on the wall, seven shelves of military archive material, and five dented silver mugs from which we'd been drinking milk or water while she'd been sipping gin.

Denise picked up one of the mugs, turned it over and peered at the silversmith's mark on the underside.

'Hm,' she said, impressed. 'This one's genuine Georgian. You could probably get quite a little something for this.'

Mary took it back from her. 'Actually, it was from my godmother and it's not for sale.'

'Mine's not either,' said Alfred George, clutching his tightly to his chest.

Denise popped Felicity's and Blanche's mugs into her bag. 'I'll take these anyhow and see what they're worth.' Then her attention was caught by a sparkle from Veritas's finger. 'Why yes!' she said. 'That's just the job. That'll do beautifully. Real diamonds and a ruby. That'll pay his fees for at least a year.'

Veritas hesitated over taking the ring off her finger. 'You

see, when he gave it to me, we always agreed that we'd pass it on to our son, when we had one, when he was old enough, so that he could give it to his fiancée.'

'Is it an heirloom then?' Denise demanded.

'Not exactly.' It had belonged to our father's elder brother. He'd saved up for it and was going to give it to his bride-to-be once he'd found one. But he'd gone and fought in Flanders, got killed and had no chance to fall in love, let alone find himself a bride. So the ring got given to his younger brother.

'Doing the right things now is more important to Alfred George than mere sentiment. And besides, it's like giving it to him if he's going to benefit from going to the right school and meeting the right people.'

Blanche and Felicity didn't see their silver mugs disappear into Denise's bag. They were still tangled up with the dogs sound asleep on the floor. It was high time they were in their cots. I carried them one after the other upstairs. Alfred George was behind the armchair, forcing himself to stay awake. He didn't want to be taken to bed.

'The head of the family doesn't have to be helped,' he said, slurred with sleep. 'Uncle Kestrel told me.'

Mary managed to chivvy him upstairs anyway. Now that our mother had to play our father's role and make important decisions (until Alfred George was old enough to do it), we had to play hers. Not just the filling of fuel hods, the chopping of kindling wood, the cutting of the grass, but also the mothering of the younger ones. In readiness for the time in two years when she'd at long last be old enough to have a driving licence, Mary had started practising driving the van round the lawns and reversing it round the hen coops.

We persuaded Alfred George into the boys' bedroom with its six beds, five of them empty, even though we failed to persuade him into bed, let alone into pyjamas. He closed the door firmly on us. Perhaps he was shy, though what did an eight-year-old have to be shy about? Perhaps he was shy of letting us see that he slept with our father's shoes beside him on the pillow.

I said to Mary, 'I'm not sure I trust her. What if she takes the ring as well as the mugs, pretends to get them valued and then sells them and never comes back?'

Mary said, 'Oh I think I trust her in that. She wouldn't get much for it. It's not as valuable as she thinks. No, it's her plans I don't trust.'

Just then, we heard a commotion in the dark outside. We peered out through the leaded panes and saw a black cab stuck sideways in the lane, its front jammed into the bank, its rear hooked on to a five-barred gate. The driver was trying to reverse into the muddy gateway through which the dairy herd processed twice a day.

It was the first time I'd ever seen a London taxi down our lane. It was, of course, for Denise, who obviously didn't intend to risk getting marooned overnight in the winter countryside when all the ambience had gone. Having sorted out our lives, Cinderella in her shocking pink Schiaparelli made sure she was whisked speedily back to the dry pavements and bright street lights of Mayfair.

Downstairs in the study, Veritas sat smiling contentedly into the embers of the fire. Mary was right. She probably missed our father just as much as I did, only in a different way. I hoped she was thinking about him now.

'Goodnight Mum,' I said, giving her flushed pink cheek a kiss.

'Goodnight Ruth. And wasn't that fun, with Denise?'

'Er, well sort of,' I said. Thanks to the gin, she obviously couldn't see the crackpot side of Denise and her plans but I reckoned that, by morning, she'd have a bad headache and be seeing sense. 'By the way, Mum, that stuff Uncle Kestrel said about us needing a head of the family, it wasn't true was it? We don't really need one, do we? Can't we make any decisions that need making together?'

'Yes Ruthie, I'm sure we can,' Veritas said dreamily.

'And another thing, Mum, that boarding school talk about Alfred George, you didn't mean it, did you? Because back in January you said that whatever happened, we should all stick together.'

'We are sticking together, Ruth. Look at us, we are.'

Of course we were. Why should I have doubted it?

'And Father is still with us too, in spirit,' she said.

And Father's engagement ring was still glinting on her finger as though to prove it.

I went to bed as happy as if I too had been drinking gin. Even my grandmother cat was content, stretched out on the counterpane, suckling her huge kitten-cat. He was a tom and guzzling greedily.

ELEVEN

Dancing Days

Veritas did not need any Alka-Seltzer. The visit and the gin had done her a lot of good. By the time I was gobbling down a bowlful of Post-Toasties and trying to finish off my homework (Latin and very hard), Veritas had already completed two hours' work at her typewriter, and begun selecting dress patterns. She'd also arranged for her ring to be taken via Cousin Roland, who happened to be popping up to town, to Denise's flat so that it could be taken to Bond Street to be valued. She'd also started sorting out some dancing class tuition.

'Dancing lessons?' I said. 'Who for?'

'You and Mary.'

'Why?'

'You won't be much use going to those dances to meet men if you don't know how to dance, will you?' she said.

I pulled down my navy blue felt hat, wrapped my stripey school scarf round my neck and pedalled fast to catch up with Mary. I was beginning to think it might be safer at school. At least my troubles there were predictable.

Alfred George didn't seem bothered about the plans afoot on his behalf. He was more preoccupied with a bird-watching hide he was building in the middle of a bramble thicket.

After school, after helping Mary shut up the hens, and after filling the coal-hod, I cornered Alfred George in his thicket. I challenged him about the future plans. 'D'you really want them to do this to you?'

He shrugged. 'Don't mind,' he said nonchalantly. 'Here, Ruth, can you hold that bit of string, while I tie this end? Thanks.' It was one of his own knot inventions. Some invention, I thought, if it needs two pairs of hands.

'But d'you really not mind if they send you away? You wouldn't be able to wear funny clothes. You'd probably have to get used to wearing dreary uniform like the rest of the world.'

'Be nice to have a few boys to muck about with.'

'There's boys here. Every holidays. Loads of them.'

'Yeah, but they're not here now, are they? They're not here at the times when I actually need them.'

'Well, I jolly well hope if it does happen to you, you make the most of it because if you don't—' But I wasn't sure what would happen if he got sent away and didn't make the most of it. That sort of thing had never happened to anybody in our family before, except perhaps in World War One when our father and his brothers had gone far away to fight. But they hadn't been sent. They'd gone of their own accord.

Alfred George was far too busy with his knots to be worried about the future. He wasn't listening to anything I said.

Personal Journal

A.G.'s right. Think Denise the menace must be a bit right too. No boys of any useful ages for any of us round here. In fact, that's the only reason I'm agreeing to go along with this dancing class stuff. Mrs Rat is pregnant again.

Mary and I had such a very long way to go to become unrustic that Veritas enrolled us for intensive tuition. Twice-weekly. Tuesday and Thursdays. After school, we pedalled reluctantly away from the direction of home and into town to Miss Silvie's large empty room on the first floor above The Railway Tavern. We had to enter round the back, past the bins, because four-fifteen was outside pub licensing hours so the main door was locked.

We propped our bikes against the fire escape and climbed the outside stairs. Mary was limping slightly even before we'd begun the dancing. She said she'd sprained her weak ankle again. It didn't look swollen so I thought she might be making it up to get out of having to dance.

'You should have brought your elastic sock,' I said.

Miss Silvie wore a calf-length Gor-Ray skirt, a scarlet wrap-around bolero top, and gold strappy high-heeled shoes. Her legs were bronzed. She had a very straight back.

'You should have brought your pumps,' she said sternly.

Mary and I looked blank. Whatever were they?

'You won't be able to dance in those walking shoes.'

'We don't have pumps,' said Mary.

'Bring them next time,' said Miss Silvie.

'I don't expect we ever will have any,' I said.

'Court shoes then.'

I said, 'We only get new shoes when we've outgrown the last pair. Our grandmother buys them for us.' Mary nudged me to keep quiet. Only very rustic girls would let on how tight things were at home.

'Very well, dears.' From then on, the first five minutes of each session was spent sticking shiny sellotape on to the soles of our lace-ups to make them slippery.

Miss Silvie pointed out to us, so we would see how modern she was, that music was provided by an electric gramophone. The turntable rotated without needing to be wound up between records. Miss Silvie's other credentials were framed and hanging in the lobby, one certificate of a dance-examination passed and, more significantly, lots of glossy photos of someone very like her but with even thinner and more highly arched eyebrows, dancing in gauze and sequins.

Miss Silvie told us she could teach us rumba, samba, mambo, tango, tarantella, cha–cha–cha, flamenco, how to dance eightsomes, foursomes, and a swirl of others. 'But your mother assures me the famous three will be sufficient for the time being. So we'll concentrate on waltz, foxtrot and quickstep. I'll throw in Sir Roger de Coverley and Dashing White Sergeant so you'll have the rudiments of the reel under your belts.'

Reels, we gathered, were dances when everybody joined in together so were essential for mixing and meeting men. Smiling all the time was important too.

'Whatever her insides feel like, a girl always keeps a happy smile on the outside,' said Miss Silvie, smiling tenaciously as we took it in turns to shuffle around in her arms.

Overhead was a glaring fluorescent light. The walls were more glamorous, hung with floor-length strips of silver foil which wafted up in the draughts as we waltzed by.

Since there were no other students, she had to partner us, turn by turn. She took the male role, steering us backwards and nudging our legs sternly with hers. She never stood on our toes though I stepped on hers quite often. She just kept smiling.

Miss Silvie taught us the cryptic language of ballroom. We had to chant it aloud like Latin declensions.

Back-side-forward-together.

One-two-slide-four.

One-two-pause-halfturn.

It was a harder language than Latin because there were no rules. The student who wasn't dancing stood against the wall and learned by watching. I watched Mary shuffling backwards as rigid as a cheese-grater.

Once we had mastered the basics, Miss Silvie tried to make us dance with each other, to take turns to be the male who went forwards and did the steering. But Mary refused.

'It's not natural. I don't like that kind of touching.'

'But she's your little sister.'

'That makes it even more unnatural,' Mary muttered through gritted teeth.

We never met other students either leaving as we arrived or waiting their turn at the end of the session. But then we didn't hang around to see. Mary couldn't wait to get home. She had to see about her pedigree piebald rats.

'I don't think she's a teacher all the time,' Mary said as we thumped our bikes into the barn. 'I think she's a lady of the night.'

'Ah,' I said. I wasn't sure what that meant. But I guessed from her stern expression that it wasn't something girls seeking allure should talk about. I wished I knew as much of the seamy side of life as Mary did. But I didn't like asking questions for fear of showing up my own ignorance.

Mary raced up to her bedroom to see how many rats there now were. Against all the odds, since they lived in separate cages, they'd begun breeding. Against nature too as sons mated with their mother, and brother with sister. From the original pair, Mary now had fifteen. The cages were on every surface, shelf and window ledge of her room. Sometimes when Mary was out at school, some of them broke out and scampered freely around the room. This was probably when the unnatural matings occurred.

Mr Rat, the male of the original pair, remained her favourite. 'He smiles at me in a kinder way than most humans,' Mary said. She carried him about, draped round her neck like a sleek muffler.

'For self-protection,' she added. 'He only attacks my enemies.'

She was gentle and wise. Why should she have any enemies? In fact, her only enemy was Mr Rat. He wanted to bite her just as much as he wanted to bite anybody. As she was putting him back into the cage from which he'd escaped, he finally got his chance. He embedded his yellow pointed fangs into her index finger so deeply that even he didn't know how to let go. Mary stared, transfixed, as he dangled from her hand, his ruby red eyes looking as desperate as hers, while her blood flowed from the wound. Mr Rat's normally beige and white pelt turned slowly pink.

I was too shocked to move. Luckily, the eggman had just called. Mr Rat's jaws had to be prised apart before Mary's finger was released. Mary stayed wonderfully calm and apologised to Mr Rat when the attack was over. I admired her.

At the start of the Easter holidays, the scrambled egg on toast, and toast and dripping regime was overthrown. Sides of beef, whole hams, ice-creams and roast potatoes daily came back in. Veritas announced that; instead of the usual children's party which she organised every holiday, there'd be a Young Person's Dance.

'Then you and Mary can put your new skills to good use. You can choose a paper pattern from the book and make yourself lovely new frocks.'

'We need shoes. Miss Silvie says you can't dance in lace-ups.'

'We'll buy some.'

Where was the money coming from?

'Oh we'll manage,' she said airily. 'Denise says I must think of investments for the future.'

'How long's this dancing got to last?' Alfred George asked, irritated. 'Because I've already got other arrangements started.' He was planning an outdoor circus with rodeo. He didn't want any would-be rope-throwers and lassooists distracted from his kind of entertainment by our mother's.

'Gloriously late. As late as anybody wants,' Veritas said, flinging her arms wide to show how late. The usual rules of liberty would apply except that everybody in the household, little boys included, must dress up in their Sunday best with ties, if they wanted to come. Alfred George still didn't seem convinced so Veritas tempted him by saying that when he was tall enough and his shoulders broad enough, he'd love dancing because he'd able to wear our father's evening suit. 'And when we were young we used to dance till dawn and then listen to the birds singing their morning chorus.'

'So till midnight then?' I said.

'Later, if everybody's enjoying themselves.'

Alfred George said, 'What's the point of it?

'Simple, straightforward, unadulterated youthful fun,' said Veritas.

I said, 'Who will we dance with?' The boys in the household were making it clear that the rodeo had more attraction. Mary didn't think much of dancing with other girls.

'Young men of course.'

'But we don't know any,' I said.

'I've invited some. Sussex is full of eligible young men,

exactly the type Denise says you ought to begin meeting. They're all simply yearning to dance with pretty young things like you. You'll have to make sure you do look pretty of course. And Mary, you'll have to try and manage without that elastic sock. It's not at all fetching. It'll put people off.'

The older girl-guests were intrigued about the prospect of a Young People's Dance, even Boodor. Although she didn't think her father would approve of her dancing closely with strangers, she joined in with getting ready.

On Dance Day morning, we rolled up the carpets in the drawing room and dragged them out to the barn. We heaved the piano into a corner, and shifted the sofa and chairs into the hall. None of the boys took any notice, let alone offered to help.

'But it doesn't matter,' said one of the au pair girls. 'Because your mother has promised real men to dance with.'

Mary couldn't help with any of the preparations. Her index finger had turned purple and gone septic. It was in a rigid plaster. Her arm was in a sling. She seemed relieved that she might not be able to dance.

Without furniture, the drawing room looked as bleak as Miss Silvie's upper room. So we picked daffodils, forget-me-nots, and fluffy cow parsley from the meadow and arranged them enthusiastically in vases. They looked so fresh and dewy. But I could see that, through Denise's eyes, they were the wrong kind of flowers.

'They give the wrong ambience,' I said. 'Too rustic. They'll have to go.'

So we substituted the flowers with red crêpe paper wrapped round the light bulbs to give the room a soft romantic glow after nightfall.

'If it doesn't catch the house on fire first,' said Cook.

Next, we set to work on hands and knees, polishing the warped worm-holed oak floorboards, rubbing in orange wax with old rags. The old boards remained just as rough and splintery.

'Try talc,' suggested Pauline. 'That's what they use at my mummy's school for the staff dance.'

We sprinkled Almond Blossom, French Fern, and Midnight Fire talcum powder till the room smelled like a beauty salon and looked as though it had a layer of volcanic fall-out.

Dumpy Cook popped out of the kitchen to come and admire our work. She was preparing the massive cold buffet supper with cider cup and lots of little things in aspic sitting on bridge rolls. In her overall and cap, she danced a quickstep round the room with her even dumpier daughter.

'Quite smooth enough, girls,' she said. 'You don't want to go making it any smoother or you'll all be slipping over and breaking your ankles. Then you'll end up in plaster and you won't be doing no more dancing for weeks.' Cook usually managed to see the worst outcome.

We spent the afternoon lying on each others' beds with egg-white on our faces and slices of cucumber cooling our eyelids, as recommended by the beauty editor of one of the magazines from under my bed. Then we ironed our petticoats, mended our suspender belts, put on clean underclothes. The girls with short hair set it with dozens of metal kirbygrips which, according to the step-by-step guide in the magazine, would make them look as regally lovely as Princess Margaret. Those of us with long hair made each other chignons, French rolls, buns and pleats. Loose hair, even to the shoulder, would look too childish for a Young Person's Dance. At seven o'clock we took it in turns to take baths made scrunchy with bath salts. Boodor brought out caskets of French and American make-up which she let everybody try.

I still hadn't quite finished making my new frock. The hem was only tacked. Would anyone see? Would it catch in the heel of my shoe as I foxtrotted backwards? I didn't mind. I felt surges of excitement like forked lightning rushing through me. I didn't know why, or what I was expecting. I just knew that this evening was going to be so wonderful it wouldn't matter any more what happened in the future.

TWELVE

And Non-Dancing Nights

At five minutes past seven, we trooped downstairs. Nothing had started happening. We tweaked at the red crêpe paper. We shivered. The boys in their grey flannel school suits and the little girls in party frocks went skidding about on the dance floor as though it was an ice-rink. Mary went back upstairs to fetch Mr Rat. She wore him for the rest of the evening, draped round her neck.

At ten past seven, Cook laid out the cold buffet supper on trestle tables in the hall. At a quarter past seven, Veritas poured some sherry into a cut-glass decanter and put it on a tray with seven nearly-matching glasses in the study.

'Who's that for?' I asked. I didn't think young people, however sophisticated, drank dry sherry.

'The parents.'

'I didn't know you'd invited any parents.'

'I haven't. But a few may have to come to bring quests who aren't old enough to drive themselves. I'll need to offer them something.'

At twenty past seven she drove down to the village to fetch the man with the music. Mr Sergeant was a retired army batman. Most of the year, he was caretaker of the Village Hall. But he could be hired by the evening to open front doors at cocktail parties, hand round champagne or, in this instance, be Master of Ceremonies. If Mr Sergeant was coming, I knew this was going to be a real dance.

Mr Sergeant wore a pre-war dinner suit, black and very formal with satin lapels on the jacket, and patent leather dancing shoes, shiny as black glass, and a clipped military moustache. He brought with him his own wind-up gramophone and a suitable selection of 78 records. He dusted them and laid them out on a folding table in the order in which he would play them. It was like watching a priest preparing the Holy Communion host.

He lent the occasion exactly that firm masculine authority which our household was supposed to be lacking. At twenty minutes to eight, he joined Veritas (in her Snow White red velvet with the fur trimmings) and Cook (in vitriolic pink nylon), to sip a small sherry in the study.

Aunt Speranza's daughter, Cousin Faith, had been invited to stay for the dance. It would've been a whole load better if her brother Tern with the sea-blue winking eyes had come instead. Faith scoffed at all our preparations with cucumber and egg-white.

'It's cissy,' she sneered. At five past eight, when the first knock was heard at the front door, she retreated upstairs, scowling. I followed her. She hunched on her camp-bed (formerly *my* camp-bed; I now had a leaky Li-Lo on the floor) with a book and a banana. I begged her to come down.

'Not likely,' she said. 'It's too terrifying. I bet Auntie V's going to make everybody play party games. Dad said she would.'

'Of course she won't. It's not a party. It's a Young Person's Dance.'

The first guest was the doctor's daughter. She had goose-pimpled arms like the rest of us.

Mr Sergeant took up his post behind the table. He announced the first number.

'Please take your partners for the quickstep, with the Sid Butler Dance Orchestra playing their well-loved *Silvered Steps*.'

Before the needle had touched the first groove in the bakelite, the young boys of our household scuffled from the drawing room and began devouring the cold buffet. They'd never had any intention of keeping their promises of one dance each.

So, after the quickstep, Mr Sergeant and Cook slid round the talcumed boards in a staid hesitation waltz. Despite their straight faces and stiff arms, I could see they were trying to demonstrate what fun formal dancing could be.

Other guests arrived in dribs and drabs, mostly more girls with shivery arms. A very few nervous youths were delivered by their mothers. Stoically, Mr Sergeant went on putting on records and announcing dance numbers. Some of us stood against the walls. Others huddled in a corner where the red crêpe paper shed less light. One thin pale person inched his way imperceptibly towards the door and gained his freedom in the hall with the younger boys.

At first, I longed to be asked to dance, even by Mr Sergeant or Cook. It was clear that none of these tense young men would pluck up the courage to ask. After a bit, I longed merely to be able to escape and hide. But by now I was glued to the wall, hands twisted like wisteria shoots behind me, unable to cross the empty floor in front of everybody. My arms were cramped. My neck ached from holding up my head. Two suspenders were digging into my thighs. My cheeks felt they would crack from the strain of keeping on the smile that would have made Miss Silvie know she'd earned her guineas.

I saw the shadow of Cousin Faith creep downstairs in my dressing-gown. I saw her retreat with an entire bunch of bananas.

Mary was not so miserably glued to the walls as the rest of us. She had the comfort of Mr Rat, hidden in the nape of her neck beneath her drooping hair-do. She went and alerted Veritas to the terrible situation. Veritas and Mr Sergeant began to organise musical games to break the ice. The small children joined in with gusto. The atmosphere improved.

Then, suddenly, new guests were arriving, not delivered by a mother but in their own noisy back-firing car. They were not shy people, but four loud young men in real dinner jackets, with slicked-down hair, and two large county girls in short tulip-skirted dance frocks. Now, at least, there was a possibility of a partner in a Paul Jones.

The four young men had deep baying voices. The two girls

shrieked. One of the men greeted Veritas by her first name, and gave her a peck on the cheek.

They called Mr Sergeant by his Christian name too.

'Harry! Simply spiffing marvellous. I say, Harry, old chum, how about some nursery rhymes? What?'

Then they danced with each other in a huddle and fell over on purpose. The girls were showing their petticoats and the tops of their stockings. I was so embarrassed I shut my eyes and pretended I wasn't there.

I knew from my grandmother that when a young man goes to a dance at someone's home, he's supposed to ask the daughter of that house for at least one dance, however ugly, lame or spotty she is. These four young men didn't even notice I was there, let alone ask me for anything. They went on romping noisily with their two big maidens, then ambled through to the study. They helped themselves from the sherry decanter while Veritas was upstairs supervising the little ones' bedtime.

Next, they moved out to the hall to laugh at the buffet. Were these horrible people really the kind that Denise thought we ought to be meeting?

'Jelly!' one of the girls shrilled. 'They've even got jelly! Haven't had jelly for simply yonks!'

'Jelly, jelly, jelly!' they chanted together and collapsed laughing.

They didn't have to eat the jelly. It was meant for the little ones. If they didn't like it, I wanted to tell them, they could have Cook's tuna mousse, or cold rice with sweetcorn, or cheese n' pineapple cubes on sticks, or chicken vol-au-vents. But by now they were hurrying into their sheepskin jackets and trilby hats.

'Try Giovanni's, shall we? Might see a bit of fun there, what?'

Of course Denise was right. I was completely rustic, and lacking any ambience or allure. I prised myself from the wall of the drawing room of my own home and slithered upstairs. Cousin Faith was still awake, sitting up with *Anna Karenina* and surrounded by banana skins. More were flopping limply over my Li-Lo.

'You're so lucky, Ruth,' Faith said. 'We never have bananas at home. Mother says they're far too expensive.' Faith's father was an officer in the navy. Surely he could sometimes afford bananas. Faith finished a chapter and closed her book with a loud slap.

'So?' she demanded. 'The dance? And what happened? Did anybody kiss you?'

'No, of course not,' I said sharply.

'What was the point of it then?'

'How should *I* know? It wasn't *my* idea.'

But for all the horror of it, the dance acted, as Denise claimed it would, like some kind of a signal, as clear as any announcement in the personal column on the front page of *The Times*. Mary's alluring existence had been noticed. Or perhaps it was Mr Rat who'd been noticed. A young man telephoned Veritas to ask permission to take Mary out for the evening.

'Isn't that nice of Roderick?' said Veritas warmly, when she passed on the invitation.

Mary didn't seem to think so. 'What am I supposed to do with him?'

'Be your own bright, lively self,' said Veritas. 'You'll chat to each other and to the other young people you meet.'

'What about?'

'You'll probably find you have simply loads in common once you get started.'

'We didn't last week,' Mary said. 'He didn't speak all evening.'

'Men can be shy too. You have to meet them halfway. Try talking about animals. I expect he's fond of animals if he remembers your rat so well.'

'Actually, he didn't even know it was a rat. He thought it was part of my chignon falling down.'

In preparation for her first date, Mary would not put egg-white on her face, or cucumber slices on her eyes. She slouched around all day scowling. One of the au pair girls, who'd recently joined the household for a summer stay, had to get her ready. Martine put down her cigarette and for the first time since her arrival became quite animated. She pulled Mary's long fluffy hair back into a tight French roll so that there was no place to secrete so much as a newborn mouse, let alone a fully-grown pedigree rat. Martine borrowed Boodor's treasure trove of make-up and dabbed rouge on Mary's cheeks and ear-lobes. This wasn't a beauty tip I'd ever noticed reading in any British women's magazine.

The suitor wore white flannel trousers and a striped blazer. He did not need his mother to drive him about. He was just about old enough to have his own vehicle, not a sports car but a small delivery van.

'The old girl's a sight cheaper to run than one of those wretched MGBs,' he explained to Mary, who instantly started looking the other way so as not to make eye contact. 'See, no windows in the back. So it's on a lower taxation level. Good wheeze, eh?'

Boodor, Martine, Pauline, Cook, two of the nannies, Veritas and I were all standing around in the drive. He seemed unperturbed by this huge send-off.

'We're going over to the rally at Hurstfield,' Roderick called out of the window to Veritas.

'Rally?' said Veritas. 'Are the cars very fast? Do take care.'

'Haw haw haw!' said Roderick. 'Nice one, mater. No, the Outdoor Folk and Country Dancing Rally. Should be rather jolly. Loads of chaps and chapesses. We might be late. All right, mater, if I don't bring her back till round about eleven?'

'Lovely,' said Veritas, waving both arms in a broad blessing. I saw Mary sink lower into the front seat till her pale face (apart from the rouged ear-lobes) scarcely showed above the dashboard.

'Oops, nearly forgot! Bring your pumps, Mary. You'll find they've got better grip for folk. Not so slippy on the grass.'

'Don't wear pumps,' Mary growled. 'Weak ankle.'

'Tennis shoes?'

'Don't play tennis.'

'Oh heck then, not to worry. I say, do call me Roddy.'

They jerked cautiously down the drive and out into the lane. I scrambled up on the five-barred gate to watch till they were out of sight. My poor big sister looked like a captured medieval princess.

'Never mind, Ruthie,' said Veritas, as though she had to console me. 'Your turn will come. I'm sure it will.'

I thought, if Roderick was anything like the Jelly People, Mary was welcome to him.

I shut up the hens for her, and fed her dogs. I needn't have bothered. She was home long before the magic hour of eleven, barefoot, carrying her shoes. Her feet were all green with grass stains. Martine's tight French chignon was badly sagging.

'You're back!' I called. I hadn't heard Roderick's engine. 'Was it fun?'

Mary shrugged.

'What did you do?'

'He bought me a ginger beer shandy. Then we danced the Queen Mab's Foursome. Everybody was in white shorts.'

'Where is he?'

'I dunno. Still there I suppose.'

'How did you get home?'

'Walked of course.'

'Hurstfield's miles!'

'Eight and a half. I would've hitched but there wasn't any traffic.' She moved swiftly off into the dark in the direction of the tool shed.

I caught up with her as she strode towards the lower orchard with a large gardening spade. 'What are you going to do?' I asked, running after her.

'We need a swimming pool,' she said grimly.

'What's wrong with the sea?'

'I don't mean for swimming in. For lounging beside. As an attraction for getting friends. The right sort. I'm going to dig one.'

'But it's dark.'

'I can dig in the dark, can't I?' she said. From the way she slung the spade over her shoulder and strode off through the apple trees, I could see that she'd prefer to dig alone.

When Veritas found out that Mary was already home and lurking somewhere in the garden, she seemed annoyed. 'Denise will be simply furious! All that trouble helping her to meet the right sort of person and she throws it away.'

In Mary's defence, I said. 'But I don't think she enjoyed the rally very much.'

'I don't expect *he* enjoyed it either, being stood up like that. It sounds as though she made no effort to be pleasant to him. You can't expect other people to do all the running, you know. You have to meet them halfway. I just hope you'll remember that, Ruth, when *you* start growing up.'

What did she mean, *when* I start?

'Yes Mum,' I said meekly. Obviously, Veritas didn't know yet what Mary was up to in the vegetable garden.

Trying to lure people in by digging a pool in among the sprouting broccoli seemed to me like going to meet them a good deal more than halfway.

THIRTEEN

Presentability

'So we're going to the palace!' Veritas announced with more than her usual enthusiasm whenever royalty was mentioned. 'That's what Denise says I must do next. Take you both to Buck Pal for the presentations!'

'The what?'

'So you can be presented to the Queen.'

I wondered why on earth the Queen would want to meet us. Veritas had been cheering up a lot lately, and when she was invited to literary events, she sometimes even went. Perhaps she'd had some exceptional success with one of her pageants which I hadn't heard about.

'Denise says it's absolutely now or never. An opportunity of a lifetime! An historical experience you'll never forget. It's the very last chance we'll get.' Veritas was urging us so keenly it sounded as if she was trying to sell blackmarket goods off the back of a lorry. Perhaps she knew I was likely to protest.

Now that our grandmother had moved into a cottage right near us, I thought she'd be a useful ally against Veritas or

Denise's wilder schemes. She disapproved of Denise and her persistent interference almost as much as I did. But, strangely, when Granny heard about the latest development, she was thoroughly in favour.

'Why, my dear Ruth, what larks for you all. Your dear mother hasn't popped up to town in ages, has she? And you two girls are definitely looking a bit peaky. I'm sure you could do with a nice day out. Remind me to give you the money for your shoes.' Twice a year, she still bought us our school lace-ups. She said it was so that our feet wouldn't grow deformed from wearing pass-ons. 'If there's one thing I can do for my granddaughters, it's make sure they have nice feet.'

Granny explained how she'd been presented at Court fifty years before, how she'd had to wear a long white satin gown like a wedding dress, three white ostrich feathers on her head, white silk buttoned shoes, and a three-foot long train.

'And it had to be exactly the right length. You'd never believe it, but the footman measured them to make sure.'

'A twain?' said Blanche, mystified. 'In a palath?'

'Not a steam train. Granny means a long bit of extra skirt that drags behind you when you walk.'

The dimensions of each part of the outfit were precise. Feathers too tall, trains too long, or a bouquet too large, and it would have looked as though the young lady was getting above herself. Too short a train, or too few feathers on the head and she was not showing the correct respect for her monarch.

Granny said, 'And they do such lovely teas at the palace. I

remember the meringues. Real fresh cream inside. So of course you must go.'

Granny's attitude to the need for regular school attendance was not as committed as her concern for our feet. A day off here, a week there, what did it matter? We were bound to get married some day so what use was all this extra book-learning?

Mary said, 'Don't forget, she never went to school. She had a governess, so how can she understand the point of Biology and Geography and the other stuff?'

Veritas's excuses for school absences were different. She believed that going to private views of art exhibitions, to first nights of plays by people she or our father once knew, to cocktail parties, where we might meet, or at least glimpse, a nearly famous person, were more educational than time spent in class tracing maps of fiords or fiddling with Logarithm tables. A visit to the palace would be the most educational trip of all. 'It'll be like living history,' she said.

Denise turned up with a new catalogue of paper dress patterns. It was bigger and glossier than the last one.

'I've brought the *Vogue* for you, darlings. There's some delicious little *haute couture* numbers at the front. I thought they'd be better for the palace. *Simplicity's* just a teensy bit common, don't you think?'

The styles that Denise thought appropriate had strange ruchings, drapes, bunched-up bodices with cummerbunds and inset gatherings.

'This is what most of the debutantes are wearing this season,' she said.

They looked to me more like soft furnishings for sofas than clothes for growing girls.

'Obviously, it's a pity you can't have a proper season, Mary. Your mother couldn't possibly afford it and anyway you're not titled. But a showing at the palace might do the trick, especially if you manage to get your picture in the paper. Not the *Mirror*, whatever you do. Maybe the *Telegraph* or the *Express*.'

As soon as the rumour of a royal visit reached him, Cousin Roland came sniffing round again. He claimed it was because he needed to borrow back the fiver he'd lent Veritas a month earlier. I borrowed two shillings from Veritas's purse on the kitchen dresser to pay for Roland's taxi, and he collapsed on the first chair he reached, red-faced and exhausted by his ride from the railway station. He patted his knee. I edged back. He was far too old to have me sitting on his lap, and so was I. He persisted in his hope that Veritas would find him irresistible. He seemed to believe that the way to her heart was via me and I was reasonably prepared to listen to him because he very occasionally gave me five bob if he'd won something on the horses. Usually though, he hadn't.

'It's all Denise's idea,' I explained, standing well back. 'She says we've got to become debutantes for a day. But I don't really understand what it's all about.'

'Then I'll tell you, m'dear.' Roland's account of the archaic practice of presenting young women at court wasn't as straightforward as Veritas's.

'You see, m'dear, it was started by young Victoria. There she was, such a lovely queen, nineteen years old, stuck at home, so much responsibility and no nice gals of her own age. She said as much to one of her ladies-in-waiting. "Why ma'am," says the lady, "My own daughter is your age exactly. She'd make a very pleasant companion."

"Definitely not!" replies Victoria, all hoity-toity. "How could your daughter be suitable company for someone like me? I've never been introduced to her." So all the lovely ladies-in-waiting had a pow-pow. How I wish I'd been there! Then they took all their delicious daughters, along with their delectable nieces, to afternoon tea with Victoria. She made the inspection herself, saw a nice bunch of fillies, definitely gals of her own class, picked the ones she took a fancy to, to be her pals till she met her Albert. He, poor chap, died of the typhoid at forty-two, even younger than your papa.'

Why did the nice men like Prince Albert and my father die and the creepy ones like Roland live on?

''Course,' Cousin Roland concluded. 'Whole thing's got quite out of hand since then. Don't know what that Denise thinks she up to. Daughters of industry and all sorts of riff-raff climbing on to the band-wagon. Your mama's different. She's got what it takes. She's really got class.'

Did a rector's daughter who couldn't pay her heating bills really have more social standing than a rich industrialist's daughter? And even if Cousin Roland's touching tale about Victoria were true, it seemed unlikely that our current queen, Elizabeth II, married, with two little children, could want to have immature schoolgirls thrust upon her for company.

'Nonsense!' said Veritas. 'She adores meeting new people.

That's what her position's all about. A good socialiser. Takes after her mother. Why, during the Blitz, the King and Queen were always popping out to chat to the locals.'

Once Veritas started reminding herself of her busy days in World War Two when she'd been driving army ambulances through the bombs, there was no stopping her. I slunk away upstairs to grapple with the fiords, leaving Roland, Blanche and one of the latest batch of kittens to absorb the rousing memories of the past. I still didn't see how the royal presentations could improve anybody's marriage prospects.

There were still many strict rules about them though they weren't written down in a rule book which a lady could consult. She just had to know and knowing was evidence enough that she was a suitable person, bringing suitable persons.

To get a royal command to attend, a lady had to write an application to the Lord Chamberlain. If he found her classy enough, he sent off the gold-edged card.

Ours came up the lane inside the canvas sack on the postman's front bicycle carrier. Veritas propped it up on the mantelpiece against the carriage clock which didn't keep good time but had been our father's, so stayed.

'You know Mum,' I said. 'I've been thinking about this presentation thing. It might've seemed a good idea in the olden days when Granny took you—'

'Olden days?' Veritas interrupted with a low hoot like an owl. 'It was not the olden days. It was 1937.'

'Well, whenever it was. Don't you think nowadays it's all a bit out-of-date?'

Our Queen had obviously begun to think so too. This was to be the final time. From next year, young ladies of society seeking acceptable husbands could carry on with their cocktail parties and dress shows and coming-out balls, but visits to Buck Pal would be on a basis of earned rather than inherited merit.

'A much better system,' I said. 'So I'll be going when they make me into a Dame.'

But the ugly dresses that looked like gathered chair-covers had already been cut out and bits of them were lying on the kitchen table. The sleeves were hanging from coat-hangers. Medium-heeled court shoes had been bought with Granny's school shoe fund. Long leather gloves, yellow and stiff and made from the skins of baby goats, had been found in Granny's corset drawer and horribly old-fashioned hats had been borrowed from posh neighbours.

'So you see, it's far too late for you to back out now,' Veritas insisted and sent a letter to Miss Eunice Ramsbottom, M.A. (Oxon). It did not request a day off. It made a proclamation that one would be taken.

Personal Journal
All most confusing.
Too poor to have radiators on.
Too poor for new uniform. (Hate wearing pass-ons).
Posh enough to get command to visit palace.
Don't mind being posh but poor. But confused.
Don't understand it. Don't understand anything much.
Does not-understanding-things matter?

FOURTEEN

Debutantes' Delights

Mary tried to join in Veritas's royalist excitement by snipping items out of the newspapers and sticking them on her bedroom wall.

'To work us up into the mood,' she said. She sounded half-hearted.

'*Deb's Delights Scarcer than Ever This Year!*' said one headline. '*With so Many Debutantes going to Court There may be a Shortage of Men to Escort Them!*' But at least it implied there'd be a sprinkling of men, even if not enough to go round.

'*Last Ever Presentation Parties! This Season's Debs make History as Well as Curtsies!*

'*What a Whirl! 118 Balls have been Announced so far. More Being Fixed Every Day.*'

'So will we have to dance at the palace?' I asked.

'Of course not!' Veritas said. 'It's not the Hammersmith Palais.'

From her newspaper researches, Mary revealed that, for the proper blue-blood debs, the presentation was only a preliminary to a whole series of social events that lasted all summer long. For us, it was one day off school.

The afternoon before the palace, Veritas met me at the school entrance like a prison warder. She bundled my bike into the back of the van. She was making sure I didn't volunteer myself for any extra-curricular activities.

'Why's your mum come to fetch you?' Muriel Pogle demanded as I flung my satchel in on top of the bike. 'She doesn't usually, except when it's snowing.'

'Special birthday treat,' I said. 'I'm getting the day off tomorrow.'

'It's not fair,' said Muriel Pogle. 'Nobody else gets days off for their birthdays.'

Veritas took us to a hairdressing salon on the sea-front where a man who insisted on calling himself Monsieur André cut both Mary's plaits off and gave her a tight Princess Margaret perm. When it was my turn, he decided that fourteen was too young to lose my plaits so he twisted them into an uncomfortable knot like a coronet on top of my head. Veritas made me sleep upright on three pillows so as not to dislodge the hair pins.

At dawn next morning, we drove to Denise's flat and ate our cheese sandwiches. Then we changed into our dreadful dresses and took a bus to Victoria. We walked the rest of the way. Shiny, black, chauffeur-driven Daimlers and Bentleys with real debs in the back, swept past us. Veritas, Mary and I teetered in our silly shoes and hats past the palace guards, in through the gates and across the pink asphalt of the forecourt.

All over quickly. (Like dentist.)

Enter palace. Hand over Lord Chamberlain's card to flunkey. At end of
corridor, separation of sheep from goats. Parents go one way, us another.
Into mirrored hall. Like speech day.

Atmosphere tense. Rows of gilt chairs.

Girls on them. No talking. Given card with own name on to hold.
Like beauty queen parade.

Some people called, 'Honourable', or 'Lady'.

Glad I'm just a 'Miss'.

'What happens next?' I whispered to Mary. My hands inside
the long stiff gloves were sweating.

But Mary had no idea either. 'We better ask somebody.'

I asked the girl next to me.

She gawped in horror. 'You don't remember what to do?
How ghastly. Didn't you go to the clawses?'

'What clawses?'

'Madame Rosa's.'

'No.'

The Honourable Camilla had been attending her curtsy
classes for the past three months. Through chattering teeth,
she recited what had to be done.

'Enter Presence Chamber as directed by footman. Keep
body erect. When directly facing HM, glide left foot back,
bend knees but back straight. Make obeisance. Right hand
lower. Maintain cheerful but not familiar expression. Incline
head to HM. Rise from obeisance. On right foot glide three

steps sideways to HRH Duke. Repeat. Rise. Proceed with upright carriage and dignity from Presence Chamber.'

'And then that's it?'

She nodded. 'Rejoin parents.'

There were no men there apart from HRH Duke, flunkeys, and people's fathers in tail coats, sitting with people's mothers on gilt chairs, watching solemnly as one daughter after another curtsied to the sovereign.

Personal Journal

Nice Queen looked young. HRH looked bored.

Tea not bad. Bridge rolls w. potted meat.

Pink and yellow fancy cakes.

Chunky utility china like Lyons Corner House.

No meringues.

Still don't see how it helps anyone get a husband.

'Now wasn't that an experience!' said Veritas, beaming, as we rejoined her and the other parents for the tea. 'Did you both enjoy it?'

Then we drove home. As an extra treat, Veritas stopped on the A21 just past Bromley and bought us fish and chips.

It might all have been a bad dream except that, next day, there was a blurry picture in one of the papers with a caption about Mary and I being the youngest debs of the year.

We didn't see it. But eagle-eyed Muriel Pogle did.

'You're a show-off,' she hissed at me during Register. 'And

a liar! You told me you were just going out for a birthday treat.'

The Needlework mistress saw the newspaper picture too. 'My dear,' she said kindly. 'What a shame you didn't let me know beforehand. I could've helped with the dresses. It looked as though those side plackets and the bodice darts didn't sit quite right.'

I didn't like to tell her that it wasn't *my* bad dressmaking she'd spotted, but my mother's.

For me, the palace trip was an embarrassing hiccup which I'd soon get over. But Mary was seriously unsettled, and not in any direction that Denise wanted.

'She got it wrong. We aren't like those double-barrell people,' Mary said unhappily, as though afraid she might be mistaken for one.

'No,' I agreed. 'I jolly well hope not.'

'We never were. And we never will be. It was just a big misunderstanding.'

Personal Journal

M calls it misunderstanding.

That's her being nice as usual. Actually, it was more about bullying and manipulation by D.

V's been too much in her grip. D got hold of V when she was specially low and vulnerable. It's wrong to do this to widows when they're in a bereaved position.

What's in it for Denise?

If only we could ban her from coming here.

Denise had already decided what she thought about Mary. I heard her telling Veritas.

'Darling, I would understand if you were just a wee bit concerned about your Mary.'

'Luckily I'm not,' said Veritas cheerfully.

'But don't you think that she might perhaps be ever so slightly deranged in the head? Have you thought of sending her to a psychiatrist? I can get you the name of a very good fellow in Harley Street.'

Veritas sounded suddenly anxious. 'D'you really think that's what she needs?'

'The way she prefers the company of her pets to young eligibles. Don't you think that's rather peculiar? And that appalling business with young Roddy and the rat. His poor mother was most dreadfully upset.'

'Roddy?'

'Roderick Ponsonby-Smythe, darling. He's very eligible. His family are frightfuly well off. He could have been quite a catch if only she'd behaved herself.'

Veritas laughed. It sounded like relief. 'Don't worry. I'm sure there'll be others. There's plenty of time. She's not even sixteen yet.'

Luckily Denise was soon off on another glamour trip to New York. The voyage took six days. We could be sure there'd be a bit of quiet, at least until she reached America. Even then, she couldn't do much except send Veritas transatlantic telegrams.

FIFTEEN

Summer Sad

That summer the pollen count was higher than it had ever been. Mary and I spent the month of June sneezing, quivering, streaming and trembling. Day and night, our faces were swollen and puffy, our noses red and chapped, our throats sore and itching.

Uncle Kestrel dropped by one soft evening on his way to Plymouth, bringing a caseful of Cousin Faith's pass-on clothes for me. So much for Denise believing that all Veritas's relations were rich enough to offer financial support.

My eyes were so swollen I could hardly peek out. My lips were so slobbery I could hardly say thank you, not that I wanted to. Cousin Faith may have been taller than me, but she was thin as a pole and mostly wore long black jerseys.

'There's only one known cure for hayfever, girls,' said Uncle Kestrel. 'Find yourself a good ship, get aboard. Tell the captain to take you three miles out to sea. Then stay there till October. It's either that, or go and work down a coal-mine. My advice is to join the WRENS. It's a fine life.'

Despite the hayfever, rural life in high summer was more disturbingly beautiful than ever I'd noticed before. In other years I'd heard the cuckoo's call echoing through the woods. But it hadn't made me stop and listen as though it was music. I'd seen things growing before. But now the tenderness of green ferns uncurling in the boles of trees, buttercups shimmering in the water-meadow, dew on carrot tops, moss on the barn roof, midges jigging in the mist above the stream brought tears to my eyes.

Veritas found me leaning out of a window with streaming eyes and nose running like a river. I was watching the sun setting beyond the furthest field.

'Oh no, poor Ruthie. Not another attack of the sniffles!' she said. 'I shouldn't stay here by the window breathing it all in. Why not have a nice deep bath? Uncle Kestrel said that helps. Or bike down to the sea for a quick dip? It's a lovely evening.'

'Not hayfever. Sun.'

'Oh dear. You haven't gone and got sunstroke, have you? Let me feel your forehead.'

'Not stroke,' I sniffed. 'Set. Sunset. So beautiful. Too beautiful.'

A herd of brown cows was being driven home to the farm. They were walking sedately in single file across the distant field. The sun on their flanks glowed like golden chocolate. There might never be another sunset like this. Yet nobody seemed to have noticed it except for me. Why was it all so beautiful? What was it for? Veritas either didn't see it as I did. Or saw it and didn't understand.

I need someone to love, to share all this terrible wonderful nature stuff with.

Mary refused to meet any more non-animal-loving men. But it was too late to reverse some of Denise's other daft plans of action. Alfred George got sent away to a males-only boarding school, just as Denise had said he should. The uniform at the centre for musical prodigies made Alfred George's choice of clothing for home-wear seem almost normal. He now had to wear canary . yellow stockings under blue corduory knee breeches, and medieval-looking shirts with frilled collars. But it wasn't just collecting bits of rope or choosing his own clothes that Alfred George was missing. It was us, his six family females. He rang up with plaintive pleas for information and gossip several times a week.

He'd speak to whoever happened to answer the telephone, even me. I'd know it was him because of the silence. I'd have to wait till he'd pressed button A to let his four pennies drop and his voice was connected.

'Hello Ruthie. What're you doing?'

'Standing in the hall in a draught. I was just passing the phone table.'

'What else?'

'Nothing much.'

'What sort of nothing?'

'You know, the usual sort.'

'Describe it. Only speak quickly so you can say lots. I'm

meant to be in prep but I escaped when the master popped out for a smoke. I came up the high street to the phone box.'

'You're not running away from school are you?' I said sternly. 'Because it's costing people quite a lot for you to stay at that place.'

He'd won a scholarship for his brilliant violin-scratching but Veritas still had to find money for the peculiar clothes, and violin strings and resin.

'Oh no, I wouldn't leave on a Tuesday because it's quintets next.'

'It's what?'

'Music. Playing in a group with other boys. Some of them are ever so good. You wouldn't understand, but it's really fun too. What else is going on at home?'

'Well, I've just finished my homework. Mary's up in the barn doing some kind of a print. Mum's typing something out in the study. Twinkletoes is pregnant again. Granny's pruning her peach trees. She says she wants to espalier them. The girls are over there helping her. She makes them lovely suppers, porridge with cream, thick rice pudding out of a tin with jam.'

I ran out of things to say. Nothing was happening apart from pollen.

'Go on.' However much you told him, he always wanted more.

'We haven't been anywhere lately. Mum says we haven't got any spare money for petrol. But luckily, there's loads of bookings for next hols. We've eaten two of the hens because they weren't laying properly. What about you? What did you have for your tea? What are you doing after your quintets?'

His money ran out. The line went dead. I made a note of his call in my book of secret thoughts.

Personal Journal

Head of the Family, eh? Some head. There isn't a head of this family. We're all just floundering along. Mary's got her own thoughts. The only nearly sensible person is Granny. But she doesn't make decisions. She's just there, with a few nice tins in her larder, eg yellow cling peaches & Ambrosia rice.

When A-G used to be around at home (tying his muddly knots), I thought he was annoying. Now I know that:

1) he's been sent too far away, right over into another county the other side of London, and

2) he's having to wear clothes even more stupid than the ones M and I had to wear for curtesying to the Queen, and

3) he's missing us even more than we're missing him.

So,

4) I feel sad for him. He's still only a little boy.

Does he think about Father as much as I do? Or more? Perhaps it's worse for him? He only had eight years of a Father. At least I had 13. But it still wasn't ENOUGH!!!!!

It wasn't just the visit to London that had unsettled Mary. Lots of things were making her restless. Even a visit from a silent female photographer unsettled her in an odd way that had nothing to do with yearning for love.

148

A journalist from one of the Sunday papers came to interview Veritas because one of her pageants was going to be broadcast on the radio.

I said, 'I thought they were meant to be visual spectacles involving lots of children. They won't be very visual on radio.'

Veritas said, 'It's amazing what the BBC manages to do with sound effects these days.'

The journalist brought the photographer. While the journalist was sitting on the terrace under the wisteria, asking Veritas questions (it was the usual old stuff about how did a mother combine running a children's holiday home with a writing career, and did she think working mothers were really a good idea and wasn't it better to spend all day looking after your children – as though Veritas had any choice in the matter!), the photographer wandered about to find a good light for when it was her turn to take her pictures. In the kitchen, she saw Mary working at the table. She'd got her favourite guinea fowl, Mrs Cannibal, to sit on the table beside a dish of worms and she was doing her portrait. I thought it was disgusting. Mrs Cannibal was completely flea-ridden. I could actually see them wriggling about and jumping off on to the table.

But the photographer obviously thought it was highly interesting. She stood and watched as Mary scratched away on her drawing board with her inky pens.

'You ought to go to art school,' she said.

Nothing more. Just that. It was enough.

The single seed of advice began to germinate. It quickly

put down strong roots in the rich compost of her imagination. It grew and flourished into a bright flower-filled meadow that was bursting to get out through her eyes and hands. These days she was at it all the time, drawing, or sketching, or water-colouring, charcoaling, ink-washing. She was up early to do it before school. She did it after school. She probably even did it in school. Anything that sat still got sketched – me, Veritas, Granny, stones, sleeping cats. Anything that moved – Blanche, Felicity, trees, sky, water, dogs and rats – also got committed to paper. She even did it on the way to school. With a pad of cartridge paper balanced on her handle bars, she scribbled the rushing, blurry roadside hedges as we free-wheeled at break-neck speed down the hills.

I knew I was being left behind, not just on the country lane, but in childhood. She was speeding ahead, discovering what she wanted out of life, grasping hold of strange ideas of freedom and independence from the paradise of family life, while I could only sit and sob at sunsets and scribble confused anguish in my notebooks.

How had she managed to do so much growing-up without me noticing? I shouldn't have spent so much time being wrapped up in my own introspection. I should have been watching her closely to see how she did it.

'You could try reading a newspaper,' she said. 'Or at least tune into the wireless occasionally, listen to what they say. It's important to be in touch with what's going on out there in the real world.'

Her advice was useful. But it was too late for me to bridge

the gulf of our respective maturity that had opened between us. I was still on the sunny slopes of childhood. She was way over on the far bank, so distant I could hardly keep sight of her.

However, she must have kept a few tender feelings for a draggy kid sister because towards the end of the summer term when our exams were over, she said,

'Hey Ruthie chick, I'm going hitching on Saturday. D'you want to come too?'

'You're what?'

'Going to the music festival.'

'What about finishing the swimming pool? We haven't done any digging for weeks. Anyway, I thought you hated country dancing?'

'Not that stuff. It's jazz.'

'Oh.' I didn't know anything about jazz. I thought it might be like skiffle or even Rock and Roll.

'More like Dave Brubeck. *Take Five.*'

'What?'

'Obviously, he won't be there. But they'll play his stuff. And I want to see what's cooking.'

'See what?'

'If you do want to come, you'll need a sleeping bag, and some money. About ten shillings. I'm taking a tent too.'

'What for?'

'To sleep in of course. If we ever get time to sleep. It might rain. Even if it doesn't, it'll be dewy.'

So did this jazz thing last all night long?

'At least,' she said. 'Sometimes longer.'

'And are we going *on our own*?'

'Not exactly. There'll be all the other jazz fans. Hundreds at least, perhaps even thousands.'

How did she *know*? Was that what reading the paper and listening to the radio was all about?

SIXTEEN

New Words, New Worlds

Veritas' face crumpled with worry. 'How long are you going for?'

Mary shrugged. 'Depends how long it takes us to get there and if it's any good.'

'You're not taking Ruth too?' Veritas said, as though I was some kind of ugly pet rat.

'It'll be quite safe,' Mary said reassuringly. 'A lord is organising it. You like lords, don't you Mum? He's got a castle by the sea.'

'What's his name? Do I know him?'

'I don't expect so. And we aren't actually staying with him. It happens in the grounds.'

'Where are you staying then?' Veritas asked.

But Mary was already hurrying off down the drive with her bedding roll under one arm. I hurried after her.

When we'd hitched to within five miles of the lord's castle, Mary took off her shoes and her pink elastic support sock and put on her rave hat, a grey felt trilby of our father's.

'It's beatnik gear,' she said.

She had a hat for me too, a black bowler that had also been our father's.

The uniform helped us to get a lift right to the castle gates with a local farmer who was transporting hay bales. I was surprised he should be so helpful given how much noise and how many music-lovers were milling about. They mostly wore thin stove-pipe jeans and huge black jerseys. There was a lot of long hair, beards, and bare feet. For the first time, I was glad to be wearing one of cousin Faith's black jerseys with the extra long sleeves that covered my hands. It made me look more like one of the crowd.

Mary and I were accepted at once. 'See you later, alligator,' one of the jazz enthusiasts called.

'In a while crocodile,' Mary replied without hesitation.

How had she learned the right stuff to say?

'Hey chicks, let's groove,' said someone else. I think he meant, Will you dance? But introductions, names and backgrounds were unimportant. So was being able to do a foxtrot, or have a clearly-defined partner. People moved about in a dancing sort of way with anybody or everybody or nobody. Some sat on the ground and stared with happy smiles.

'Hey chicks, don't you dig this crazy swing, like? Yeah, yeah,' a grizzled man, who was probably smiling beneath the beard, said. He looked scary but I think he meant it in a friendly way.

'The tube really sends me,' said another.

'Hot diggety dog.'

'Hey man, this joint's cooking. They got it wired.'

'It's like way out.'

It was a strange disjointed language. Even when I couldn't understand the actual meaning, I soon got the jist of it.

It was mostly about keeping cool, yet being hot at the same time and having a detached attitude while enjoying everything. Man, chick, dig, like, cat, ball, crazy, swing, pad, square, hip, cool were key vocabulary. As night fell, the ambience got hotter and the actual temperature cooler. Dew gathered, mist wafted and our naked feet became cold and very wet. But at least I felt that we were really with it.

Outside the castle gates more bands played louder and faster than the ones inside.

'Trad,' said Mary approvingly.

'Cool, man,' I said.

The trad bands were moving in a straggling, dancing procession down a track towards the sea, playing as they went. People followed and went on dancing as though nothing would stop them. We went too. It felt like going after the Pied Piper. We reached a cove where shallow waves lapped the shore. A bonfire was lit and flamed in red and orange. The white moon came up behind the castle. The music played on. There was dancing on the sand, on the dunes and through the gentle waves, stirring up trails of luminous phosphorescence like liquid fire in the water. People danced up to their ankles, up to their knees, and even up to their waists. Mary too. Her weak ankle, I noticed, didn't seem to be giving her any pain at all.

Mary dried out by the bonfire. A man with a beard kept talking about the Ferlinghetti. I thought it must be a type of car.

'A beat poet,' Mary whispered reverently. The only poet I could think of was the lord who'd written a poem called 'Mariana of the Moated Grange' but it sounded like it might be a different kind of poetry so I kept quiet and just listened.

When we went back to our tent, we found it was full of other people. It was anyway a very small scruffy tent. Now it looked like an over-full laundry bag.

'Not to worry,' said Mary in normal language. 'They probably need it more than us. We'll sleep over here.' She carried our bedrolls to put them by the bonfire. But we didn't get a chance to sleep there either. More people arrived and began to bake potatoes in the embers of the fire. Then others came with bongo drums. Then two saxophone players made mysterious haunting sounds through till dawn.

As the sun came up over the horizon, I thought how I wanted it to stay just like this always, with the fluffy clouds and the sleeping people, and the wild grasses blowing on the dunes. And more than anything, I wanted to fall in love with someone so I wouldn't have to be alone with all this beauty.

We stayed at the festival for another day. But I was growing anxious. Although I liked it, at the same time I felt a dutiful pull. Technically, we were truanting. Reluctantly, I said to Mary, 'It's Monday. What about school?'

She said, 'I've left. Didn't you know?'

'You can't have!'

'Yes I can. I'm old enough. I'm going to art school. I took some work along to show them. The Principal said I can start next term. I'll get a grant and rent a room.'

I felt confused. How could she leave me? It felt like betrayal. Clearly, sticking by me in a bond of eternal sisterhood came low on the list of priorities. So had any desire to find a rich sleek man with a fast car. So had her plan to finish digging us a swimming pool.

Art came first.

It was a long hitch home. It took all day with a lot of waiting and walking in between lifts. Veritas was relieved rather than pleased to see us back.

'Thank goodness. There's four holiday children arrived early. Cook's not due till the day after tomorrow. And I've got to pop up to London to arrange a few things with Denise.'

She had the van piled up with some tatty lampshades, a wicker laundry basket full of faded military papers, and our father's Aboriginal boomerang poking out of the top. Usually it hung on the wall behind his desk. What was she up to? Was the financial situation so desperate that she was trying to flog a few of our father's souvenirs? And why London? And what few things to arrange?

'Just things. Be back by midnight,' she said as she jumped into the driving seat and spluttered off down the lane without explaining anything. So it was up to Mary and me to prepare the next meal and some holiday fun for our sisters and the early visitors.

For the next two months, I could put Veritas's plans out of

my mind. There were so many children and so many helpers in the house, there was no time to worry about anything. Like summer wasps and bees, the holiday children increased in numbers throughout July, they buzzed and swarmed to their peak in August. Then the frantic stage passed, and they gradually began to disperse, packed off to their boarding shools, flown away to their Swiss finishing schools, re-inserted into their step-parents' service flats.

Now, there were just a couple of lazy lingerers whose parents worked on the other side of the world.

Then Mary went away too, to a first-floor room in a boarding house on the sea-front. From now on, being a beat-chick was the nearest she intended to get to the animal kingdom. She'd already disposed of most of her livestock. Her guinea fowl and mynah bird went to the Greenfinches' farm. The rats escaped of their own accord in an unnecessary fit of panic, then leaped out of the bedroom window and disappeared.

'All dead,' said Felicity solemnly.

'No they's not,' said Blanche. 'There's no corpses.'

It had become my task to take care of her most recent aquisition, a mongrel bitch puppy, named Bounder because of her tendency to leap at anything that she thought she saw moving, whether real or imaginary. I took Bounder for frequent treks round the lanes to wear her out on the end of one of Alfred George's extra long ropes.

'Ah, you're back at last,' said Veritas, as Bounder dragged me in through the back door. 'You've been gone hours! I was beginning to wonder what on earth had happened to you. I had to do *all* the packing without you. Luckily Cousin Roland dropped by to lend a hand.'

My heart gave a lurch. Bounder took advantage of my lack of concentration to pull herself free.

I said, 'What packing?' But I knew what was coming and I didn't think I could bear it.

SEVENTEEN

The Precious Place

Why was Veritas so keen to move?

'We must ride with the tide, that's what Father always said.'

'Did he? I don't remember him saying it.'

'And everybody knows that living in Sussex is one of the most expensive luxuries in the world.'

'And London isn't?'

'Yes. So this luxury life has got to stop.'

'Which "everybody" says so? Denise I suppose?'

'Well, she did mention it.'

I said, 'And did she worry about the charcoal burners who also live in this county, in their cabins in the chestnut woods? Did she say *their* lives in Sussex are expensive luxuries? Ought they to move to a different place too?'

'Don't be difficult, Ruthie. You know what I mean. Denise got Roland to look at the accounts for me. And they both agreed that running a holiday home without Father is just too much. Denise says she's sure I'll be able to pick up bits and pieces of freelance work and I might hit the jackpot one of these days. She's heard a rumour that the BBC are going to develop their programmes for children.'

I thought, surely it's usually the children who leave home to seek their fortunes in the big bad city, and the parents who stay behind?

'Denise can't tell me what to do with my life,' I said defiantly. 'So I'm jolly well staying here.'

'Who with?'

'On my own if I have to.'

'And who'll pay the rent? Anyway, the new tenants are moving in tomorrow.'

How could she bear to abandon this precious place? Our hamlet was where everything of any importance had happened to us.

'Seriously Mum,' I pleaded. 'We can't go. It's our home. What about Father? We can't leave his grave with no one to take care of it.'

All that visiting the churchyard she'd made us do – at Easter and Whitsun, on his birthday, on the anniversary of when he and Veritas first met during the Blitz, on the anniversary of their marriage. What had been the point of all those commemorations if she was now leaving him behind?

'Graves are very unimportant places, Ruth. Compost heaps, really. The things that matter go with you wherever you are. You won't forget Father just because you aren't near the churchyard any more.'

'What about the holiday children?' I thought of Johnnie, already looking forward to spending Christmas with us, just as he had since he was five.

'The new people will have them. They're going to run it just the same, except it'll be a children's riding centre. And they've got *ponies*,' she added, as though that would make all the difference to the seasonal comfort of Boodor, and Maggie, and Rashid, and Krishnan and Gordon, Lucille, Katie and all the other regulars. 'People love riding holidays. Ponies are all the rage these days.'

I thought, But what if the children I'd grown up with didn't happen to *like* the pony people? I said, 'Well, it's definitely going to be a big shock for Johnnie, turning up to stay with us and finding it's not us after all. You ought to write and warn him. Cousin Roland's going to miss you too. And what about Cook and Pauline?' Ours was the only steady home Pauline had ever known.

'They'll be all right. I talked it through with Cook. She's moving to a new job with her own flat. It'll suit Pauline better too. She'll be able to go to a proper girls' grammar school instead of that boys' prep.'

Lucky Pauline. I used to feel sorry for her, no father, no home, no sisters. Now I almost envied her.

'There's still another thing, what about school for our little ones?' They really liked it down in the village with Miss Bodger. Blanche had managed to learn to read without the use of Miss Bodger's vigorous teaching methods, and as for Felicity, at least Miss Bodger never used the strap on the very new infants.

Denise must have talked about all this a great deal when

I wasn't listening at doors for Veritas had an answer for everything.

'They'll go to a new school. The change will do them good. They do have schools in London too, you know.'

What about the hollow oak tree halfway down the sunken lane? And the wild irisies in the stream? And the fresh water spring in the meadow? And the pale wind anemones?

'Ruthie, you soppy old thing! They don't belong to us. Nothing does.'

'I know. But we still can't leave them behind. They need us to look at them or there's no point in them being there.'

'There'll be other people to see them.'

At last, I found the ultimate objection. She couldn't possibly have a ready answer to this next one.

'There's Granny!' I said triumphantly. 'You can't leave her behind. Specially not just when the builders have begun mending her roof.' Now had Veritas thought of that?

Indeed, she had.

'I think Granny's going to be quite relieved to have a bit of a break from all of us.'

How could she have had enough of us when, out of all her eight children, she'd chosen Veritas as the one to live next to, when she'd bought the next-door field and done up the little tumbledown cottage?

'Poor Granny. Left behind, alone in her field.'

'Not poor Granny at all,' said Veritas, surprisingly sharply. 'Nobody asked her to come here. She could just as well have bought herself a cottage next door to Thrift, or Charité, or Speranza.'

Perhaps I didn't understand everything. Perhaps this was more a case of Veritas running away from her mother, and less to do with me and my mother?

It was time to go. Everything that could be, was packed in the van. Bounder was caught, and shoved into the back of the van too. She tried to jump out over the bundles of bedding and books. Blanche grabbed her collar and shoved her into a metal meat-safe that was near the top so she couldn't escape. Then Blanche squashed herself next to Felicity beside Veritas's typewriter and the filing cabinet. There was still a tiny space at the front reserved for me. But I could not make myself get in.

'Do hurry up, Ruth. We really can't hang about any longer,' Veritas said. 'The new tenants' horse-boxes are arriving any moment now. And their grooms. We don't want to be blocking the drive.'

'I'm not coming with you, Mum. Sorry.'

'Your things are already in.'

'I know. But I can't. There's all sorts of reasons. I'm not a Londoner. I don't belong there. I'm not ready to start a new life.' I unpacked my rucksack with the personal journals in it, clean knickers and socks, Tampax, pocket dictionary, Osmiroid (italic nib) fountain pen, toothbrush, and the bowl of early-flowering hyacinths I'd potted up in leaf mould ready to put on Father's grave at Christmas.

Veritas said, 'All your friends are starting new lives.'

I thought, What friends?

'There's your blue-stocking pal from school, Muriel, studying lots of subjects so she can go to Cambridge. Or is it Oxford? And Lousia who came to the dance is going to Charm School. And you must remember your cousin Fox? He's definitely starting something somewhere too.'

Of course they were all doing interesting things for they were proper people with proper lives. It was easy for them to face the autumn term. They'd got parents who'd stayed around to see they got educated, whereas I was totally improper, had no sense of direction, and nowhere to belong. Moreover, I hadn't managed to get anyone, not even a rat, to fall in love with me.

'Mum, you don't *understand!*' I wailed. But when did she ever?

Bounder, trapped inside the meat-safe inside the van, began howling desperately and scrabbling with her paws to be let out. The poor puppy didn't want to move to London any more than I did. At the same time, Mrs Twinkletoes who was supposed to have gone to live with Mrs Hare up the hill, appeared at our ankles and began wailing eerily as she tried to find a way into the van. Like Veritas and Dick Whittington, she definitely seemed to want to go to London to seek her fortune.

'So if you're not coming with us, what are you planning to do?'

I hadn't a clue. I cast my eyes up to the blue of the Indian summer sky. No clues there. Then at the golden leaves of the pear tree. And through them, a hundred yards away, I caught sight of the welcoming little windows of the cottage in the next-door field. I caught a glimpse of the variegated dahlias shouting in shades of pink and orange and mauve. They weren't exactly calling me to join them, but they were proclaiming that they were there. I saw the peach trees, espaliered into a neat line, suggesting a future of calm regularization which is what I thought I hankered after.

I saw the raffia gardening hat bobbing about at the far end of the back garden. I saw my dear old grandmother and I knew I loved her.

When Grandfather died, she'd chosen me to be her companion following the coffin. Perhaps, now that my family was disintegrating around me, I should choose her to be my companion?

I said, 'Actually Mum, I'm going to live with Granny. In her garden room.'

Veritas looked surprised. 'Really? She never mentioned anything about that to me. And her garden room hasn't got any proper foundations. It's most frightfully damp.'

'I'm strong,' I said, wondering if I was.

'Does Granny even know?' Veritas asked.

'Sort of,' I lied.

'Oh good! Then that's really wonderful! You can hold the fort!' Veritas seized, as always, upon the more positive side of a vaguely negative situation. 'You can look after Bounder. I never did feel happy about having a country puppy in a flat.' She unhinged the meat-safe and Bounder bounded gleefully out of the rear doors of the van and straight back into the house we were supposed to have just vacated.

Meanwhile, Mrs Twinkletoes leaped straight into the van and snuggled herself deep down under a pink eiderdown and began to purr with contentment.

'Don't worry, Mum. I'll go in and catch her as soon as you've left,' I said half-heartedly, knowing I didn't want to have to go back inside our old home ever again. It was goodbye to that entire bit of life. When we first came to this hamlet, we'd been a big, whole, happy family. Then turned ourselves into an ever bigger family. That was the best part and had lasted until bits of family had started breaking off.

First Grandfather. Then the cats that got run over. Then the kittens that had to be drowned. And the rats that killed themselves. And Father. And then Alfred George torn off by being sent away to posh school. And Mary taking herself off to a life in Art. Now, all that remained of our family was a small crumpled bit, just Veritas, two little girls, and a feline great grandmother.

I felt terrible. I knew I ought to stick with them. But I couldn't. I wasn't ready for a big move. All I ever wanted was for life to stay still, to remain the same. Yet it never did.

'By the way, what are you going to do?' Veritas asked.

'Dunno. Expect I'll read some more Moli're. And a bit of Voltaire. Maybe I'll write some poems. I suppose I'll go back to school. If they'll have me.' And there was a lot of catching up with the Personal Journals to be done.

'That's all very well. But what'll you live on? You know

Granny can't keep you. She's only got her church pension.'

'I'll get a job,' I said airily, as though there were suddenly going to be loads of jobs in the hamlet. 'First thing tomorrow morning.'

'Perhaps you could ask the new people? They might need a stable-hand.'

'Mum! You *know* my feelings about horses.' Or had she forgotten already?

A few more hugs and kisses and the remnants of that part of my family left. I walked across the lane and down the path to Granny's cottage, still damp despite the builders' work. I put my rucksack in the porch and strolled down the mossy lawn to where she was digging furiously in the furthest corner of her garden from where she wouldn't see and could hardly hear the sound of a departing van.

'Why, Ruth my dear!' she said, looking genuinely surprised. She slowly straightened up on her border fork. 'I thought it best not to come over and say goodbye to the small girls. I hope your mother didn't mind too much? But I've got far too much to do with getting this herbaceous border into shape before the first frost.'

Who was she pretending to? Certainly not to me. I knew what she meant. Comings and goings were just too difficult so it was better not to watch.

I explained how I'd quite like to come and live with her. 'If that's all right? I'll be very quiet. I won't get in your way.'

'Very well dear. There's not much for supper tonight. Just some sardines, and a few tomatoes. They're ripening nicely.

Though I dare say we'll manage, don't you?'

I said, 'I'll try not to eat too much.' I thought of the delicious tins of yellow cling peaches in her larder and the tinned rice puddings. I was pretty sure she'd share them.

She handed me her border fork and pointed with the toe of her galosh to a clump of growing leaves.

'Look, Ruth, d'you see the delphiniums? They're terribly congested. I've been trying to lift them. They need to be divided. Would you have a go for me while I put the kettle on?'

As I spat on the palms of my hands and started digging with my Granny's trusty fork, I tried to persuade myself that I felt perfectly fulfilled. From now on, I told myself, my life will be safe and perfectly straightforward. But then I thought of Veritas and the overloaded van trundling along towards the bright city lights. Had I really made the right choice? Had I even made any choice at all? Or had I merely settled for the easiest option of snuggling down into the nearest security?

What had happened to that spark that had once yearned for so much? If Mary could launch herself out into the world by the simple force of her own creativity, why couldn't I? I tried to tell myself that I was merely putting off till tomorrow (or the day after or next week) the decision about what I should do with the rest of my life. But I wasn't fooled.

As I got the delphinium roots divided, Bounder came trotting cheerfully across the grass towards me. That was a relief. At least I wouldn't have to go back into my old home to search for her.

Bounder looked pleased to have found me. If dogs really can smile, then I was pretty sure she was grinning with joy. Her choices in life were so straightforward.

'There's a good girl,' I said, reaching out to get hold of her collar. 'You come and sit here and I'll take you walkies later on. OK?'

Bounder wagged her tail in agreement, but as soon as she saw the piece of string in my hand that I was going to attach to her collar, she changed her mind and darted away after an imaginary rabbit.

I heard Granny calling from the cottage.

'Ruth, dear! Nice pot of tea, all hot and ready!'

I wondered, Could I really spend the rest of my life with no proper ambitions, and nobody for company but an old granny and a disobedient dog?